"A beautifully written first novel. . . . The two girls' voices are contemporary and credible, jokey and young . . . the prose is nuanced, eloquent."
—*Quill & Quire*

"*Skinny* is one gorgeous, unsettling novel. Kaslik details a volatile sisterhood fuelled by injury and recalcitrance, and while the final pages leave one aghast and saddened, there is that undeniable, heady thrill of having just spent time with a talented new writer."
—Jonathan Bennett, author of *Verandah People*

"Kaslik's last chapters bring a bitter end as engrossing as it is uncompromising."
—*The Globe and Mail*

"Ibi Kaslik is a brilliant young writer who understands the power of secrets. Her writing is sharp and true, like a knife that cuts to the bone in a single stroke."
—Larissa Lai, author of *Salt Fish Girl*

"A first novel that is vivid, compelling, at times even darkly funny."
—*Montreal Review of Books*

"A luminescent read, and the narratives—split between the protagonist sisters—reveal two spectacular landslides. . . . The book's emotional grip is fierce, and the hunger of its characters for love and understanding is compelling."
—*Eye Weekly*

"[A] profound portrait of girlhood. . . . Brutally beautiful. . . . The psychic inner worlds of both girls ring painfully true."
—*NOW* magazine

# ibi kaslik

# skinny

Harper*Perennial*Canada
HarperCollins*PublishersLtd*

*Skinny*

© 2004 by Ibi Kaslik. All rights reserved.

Published by Harper*Perennial*Canada,
an imprint of HarperCollins Publishers Ltd

First trade paperback edition by HarperCollins
  Publishers Ltd: 2004
This paperback edition: 2005

HarperCollins books may be purchased for educa-
tional, business, or sales promotional use through
our Special Markets Department.

HarperCollins Publishers Ltd
2 Bloor Street East, 20th Floor
Toronto, Ontario, Canada
M4W 1A8

www.harpercollins.ca

Library and Archives Canada Cataloguing in
Publication

Kaslik, Ibolya, 1973–
Skinny / Ibi Kaslik. – 1st digest ed.

ISBN-13: 978-0-00-639228-6
ISBN-10: 0-00-639228-8

I. Title.

PS8571.A8494S55 2005      C813'.6
C2004-907298-6

RRD 9 8 7 6 5 4 3 2 1

Printed and bound in the United States
Set in Monotype Garamond

FOR MY FAMILY

*History, like trauma, is never simply one's own. History is precisely the way we are implicated in each other's traumas.*

—Cathy Caruth, *Unclaimed Experience: Trauma, Narrative, and History*

Once, Dad stuck Holly in a tree.

We were all in the backyard, just after dinner, eating pears. Mom was sitting on the porch, barefoot, her thin red skirt folded between her knees as she skinned pears and cut them into wedges and then passed them on to me and Dad. They were warm and juicy and required hardly any chewing.

Holly was playing with sticks in the garden. She was wearing a pale blue dress. I used to like to watch her play in the garden. She always looked so calm and complete, a little lady, as she bent down to sniff lilies. Mom and I were sitting on the top step. Dad was on the bottom, shirtless and smoking a cigarette. Muscles flickered in his dark back in sculpted waves as he turned around to accept slices of pear from Mom. We were full from dinner and I was planning how I would escape to the park to ride the new ten-speed I'd received for my twelfth birthday without Holly trying to follow me on her bike. But the thought was uncomplicated and faded quickly; I decided I would ride around the street with her that night, if she wanted.

We watched Holly going from flower to flower. Her small

hands were folded behind her back and she moved with the patience of someone much older. Then she stopped and stared at the oak tree at the edge of the garden.

She pointed up and then looked back at us, insistently. Dad's cigarette dangled from his mouth as he walked over and said something to her. Holly nodded, mouthed something back to him, and grinned.

Mom and I watched his thin, tanned body framing Holly's small figure as he lifted her over his head so she could grasp a branch. He held her there until he was certain she had established a firm hold. Then he let her go.

As he strode towards us through the grass, the sound of crickets became louder. He took the porch steps two at a time and didn't turn back once. I watched his face as he pitched his cigarette into a tin can by the door and wondered if he would look back at her. He didn't.

Mom and I sat there sealed together by the warm August wind, watching the little slip of blue hanging six feet from the ground, swaying back and forth.

Holly's plaintive moan was a curious sound, not a cry of pain or worry, merely the sound of something buried, or nearly lost, and it caused Mom to snap out of the spell. She rushed across the grass and grabbed Holly by the waist. Holly fell into her embrace and giggled, as if she were the only one who understood Dad's idea of a joke.

part i

# chapter 1

Innate immunity: The human body has the ability to resist all types of organisms or toxins that tend to damage the tissues and organs. This capacity is called immunity.

Holly will always be immune from the damage that infects me so easily. She comes to visit me today at the clinic, smelling of lilacs and peanut butter.

"Where did you go?" she asks me, her clear, pale grey eyes blinking from the sun slanting through the room. She kicks up her skateboard and pulls her headband down over her eyes.

Hello, My Name Is: Giselle Vasco. I am a twenty-two-year-old recovering anorexic. Hello, My Name Is: Taking-One-Year-Out-of-Med-School-and-Starting-Again. Hello, My Name Is.

"They say you can come home now."

"I know, but do a cartwheel."

"Here?" she asks in mock surprise.

*—Here? In this waste of a place you call home?*

"Do one, and I'm yours."

I follow her to the hallway, where Mom and a couple of other nurses are standing around waiting for the elevator. I lock eyes with Mom, whose gaze is pleading but fierce.

Holly does three perfect cartwheels: arms arched and nearly straight, her body star-shaped, her mismatched socks folded over her high-top basketball sneakers, the kind all her fourteen-year-old friends are wearing.

"So, what's it gonna be?" Holly asks, wiping her nose on her wristband, her grey eyes daring me. I look down at my skinny, knobby legs that are so unlike Holly's; hers are tanned and covered in fine blond hairs, while mine are pale and stubbly and covered by razor nicks. Holly's legs are strong, muscled, a set of powerhouse tree trunks, and, if I hold on to them firmly enough, they can cartwheel me out of here.

I look back at Mom's glistening eyes.

*—Here, in this waste of a place you call—*

"Let's go home."

Medical students will be able to perform the following routine procedures: Ace bandaging, insertion and placement of venous catheters, scrubbing, sterile preparation, finger splints, radial and ulnar gutter slab, draping, and suturing of simple laceration.

Ah yes, I learned it all, immediate attention to cuts, needles, breaks, the general wear and tear of the human body, only to promptly wind up in a hospital unit myself.

Vesla, my mother, drives the car like a maniac, as if she's afraid I'll change my mind about leaving. Her speeding makes me nauseous and the wide pink and blue suburban houses of our neighbourhood blur by as I try to count them. Holly is excited, telling me all the things we'll do together, like play tennis and eat blue slurpies and camp out in a tent in our backyard.

We don't go straight home; instead, Mom pulls into the cemetery where our father is buried. When she takes the key from the car, she turns and surveys us like she used to do when we were kids, fighting in the back seat.

"You know, Giselle, your father and I came to this country so you could eat, so you could have choices. And look at you now, you look like a prisoner. You have to promise me you're going to eat with us and be good. Because this, my darlink, this is not fooling around anymore. This is nothing."

This is Mom's good English. *Darlink*. Sometimes she mixes up expressions in times of crisis. I lean over the seat to hug her head.

Mom crosses herself and gets out of the car.

We walk to the grave silently, all three of us holding hands, with me in the middle. Both Holly and I are about half a foot taller than Mom, and lighter skinned, like our father was. Mom's olive skinned, with wide cheekbones and dark Eurasian eyes. Her eyes betray her Hungarian–Romanian ancestors, from Erdély. Erdély Hungarians are famous for their remote resemblance to Asians, and for their unflagging sense of humour in the face of disaster. Though my eyes are blue, I like to think I've inherited Mom's distinct, almond-shaped eyes.

When we get to Dad's grave, Holly goes down on her knees and pats the soft earth with her hands. I look at the crucifix over my father's grave. Jesus' eternally baleful eyes are locked on a spot on the ground where Holly's hands play.

Before Holly was born I used to kneel in the dirt and pray under the soulless sunflower heads that lined the back of our garden. The balls of my feet dug into the ground and the soil yielded beneath my knees as I prayed for a dog or a brother.

I'd do twenty Hail Marys, a couple of Our Fathers, and then try to draw a picture of my future brother in my head. My mother, her long dark hair pulled back in a neat bun, would scowl at me as I came in dragging my feet and combing the black and white seeds out of my hair. She was alarmed in those days by my religious fervour.

"Please don't drag your dirty feet on the floor, Mother Teresa," she would tease, half smiling, holding her round belly. Now, at my father's graveside, looking at Jesus' down-turned eyes brings back those old feelings, but it's like seeing someone you used to be in love with and being with a bunch of people making fun of him. I understand his terror at being up there all alone, watching the perpetual unfolding drama—the way our lives get cut up by seasons and weakness and change without our noticing.

Most of all, though, I feel shame for putting my mom through this two-month ordeal at the clinic, for my shaking, sweaty hand that I have to pull away from hers to steady myself on a nearby tree. Shame for the sudden clenching in my bowels.

The macaroni-and-cheese lunch I had somersaults in my tiny gut. It's only been two weeks that I've started eating normally, so my stomach's not used to being full.

—*What's this!?*

And then I'm on my knees, and she's in my throat, churning the food into bile, interrogating, the endless interrogating.

—*Tell me, what does it feel like to almost die?*

The trend of metabolic changes occurring in starvation is similar to that after shock.

Almost, almost but not quite, you can function while starving.

I saw her in public today. It had been weeks since my last sighting. She was walking towards me on a busy downtown street: a sickly girl, pale and shivering but kind of pretty, if you like that ravaged look. Her hair was sticking out at odd angles, dry blond dreadlocks tied willy-nilly with pieces of string. I almost didn't recognize her.

She wore a leather jacket and her boys' jeans were sutured to her hips with a leather belt. Her black army boots were scuffed and she carried a thick, worn medical dictionary under her arm.

I tried to avoid her but she turned and spoke. She's always talking at me, it seems:

—*So, you never answered my question.*

—What?

—*What does it feel like?*

—Stopit.

Caught in a beam of sunlight, we both stopped walking and stared at each other through the reflective building windows. I was stunned by the image of this wasted woman before me. Myself.

Demonstrating resolve to be a well-adjusted person is a positive signal to yourself that the strain of medical school will not compromise your individuality.

Before the end of term, before I got really sick, med school was actually amazing. I kick-started out of the gate rising, like Holly. I wanted to jump into my life, one outside the drab aluminium-siding world of green lawns and moody women. I needed to get lost in the world, to pound out the thoughts of Eve, my ex, who had left for Germany that summer without promising me anything except postcards.

I'd just finished a fast-track B.Sc. in biology and wanted what I had seen in movies: friends, classes, a second degree at the end of it, a career. The image I had of my future was all straight as a Hollywood film—melancholy little suburban girl goes to university, finds herself, gets a life, a boy, a degree. Start nostalgic music, cut to me inside my tiny shared student apartment, watching the yellow-and-brown polyester curtains blowing stiffly, looking at biology books, listening to the bleached-blond girl upstairs ride her long-haired boyfriend. I am twirling my hair, am deliriously happy, grooving on this egghead high. She is me, this girl, she is Hello-My-Name-Is . . .

It was enough to hang out of the windows smoking my roommate's cigarettes, to laugh at drunken frat boys running around the street in their underwear. I was absorbing everything, and for a couple of months I got it, I was doing it. I was doing it right, all right. The classic-rock music from the frat house nearby was the soundtrack to my life.

Then, halfway through the second semester, I'd find myself walking around the campus, lost.

"Excuse me, um, could you tell me where the, ah, building with the, you know, the tower thingy . . ."

*Aphasia: Muteness, loss of speech, due to the brain's malfunction.*

"The library? Sweetheart, it's right in front of you."

I'd get flashes of hot-and-cold panic that made my body shake. I'd have to go to my room, lie down with the covers pulled over my face and wait for my body to stop trembling. Panic attacks, I guess, where I'd walk around for hours counting bones, naming body parts, muscles, diseases, doing anything to stave off the naked fear that whirled in my gut like a snake's tail, that threatened to lash out at any second and ensnare some poor unsuspecting student or professor.

Incredibly, I could still study. All I could do, it seemed, was write tests, cram every spare moment with books, notes, labs, lectures. But at night, when the girl upstairs had long since pleasured her hippie-boyfriend and the curtains looked harsh and cheap, I couldn't stay within those walls. I'd learned too much, my head was full, and the part that wasn't full would wonder about Eve. I started skipping meals now and then and had lost a bit of weight from worrying about marks. One night, bored with studying, I started prowling the bars.

"Giselle! Bloody hell! Miss Bookbrains finally got her arse out of jail!"

It was Susan, my Scottish roommate. Susan was a tall, ever-smiling, red-headed psychology major. She had a bad case of eczema on her arms, which I tried to treat with creams and poultices. Since nothing ever seemed to work, she wore long, satin gloves up to her elbows to hide what she called her "bloody leprosy."

"Hey, Suze. Whatcha drinkin'?" I asked, standing awkwardly at the edge of the table, shy about being the centre of attention. That night at the bar, Susan was sitting at a large table, surrounded by friends. It was somebody's birthday and there were pretty little gift bags stacked on one side of the table. Susan was sitting between two collegiate-looking guys, and the girls at the other end of the table were wearing little black dresses. I felt self-conscious suddenly; I pulled up my sagging jeans and pushed out my chest, trying to hide the stains on my worn tank top.

"There's a special on screwdrivers," she told me. "And we've got loads of beer, but I'm drinking whisky."

"Whisky it is then." I ordered a screwdriver for myself, and a whisky for Susan, who finagled me a seat near her next to an all-American-looking guy who introduced himself as Greg.

"Giselle's my roommate, guys . . . the one I was telling you about before. Killer marks, doesn't get out much though." Everyone at the table laughed and bobbed their heads at me as we raised our glasses.

Susan was what people call a party animal, and her lifestyle suited me fine as she usually came home about the time I left for classes with "a hangover that could make your gnarly toenails crackle." She always left a mess in her tears through the place, which I picked up after without complaint because she kept the fridge stocked with the essentials: a pack of Benson & Hedges Special Lights, Clamato, a fifth of vodka, lemon wedges, and crackers—for guests, she explained.

When Susan put her arms around me in the bar, surrounded by her friends, I rested my head on her shoulder for a second and realized that I hadn't been touched in months. I felt starved for affection, for human interaction, as Susan pulled me to her to whisper secrets.

"What do you think of our all-American golden boy?"

"I think you like him."

Starved. For salty peanuts, for beer poured in chilled mugs, for music blaring through conversations punctured by laughter and smoke. I sat next to Susan that night, trying to follow her conversations, trying to read the significance of her hand on Greg's knee.

"You're right. I want to lick him," she told me through sips of whisky as my eyes caught Greg's briefly and he winked at me.

I looked over at the girls and laughed when they threw popcorn at us. I had never tasted beer this good, heard music so sweet and true. All of my preoccupations about marks, school, main arteries, veins, lymph nodes, diagnostic methods, and the memory of Eve's kisses on my mouth slipped away for a couple of hours. I was free; this was what I had come for. The confusing mass of impulses and emotions: the wandering, the shaking and the panic, the hours I'd spent cradling huge textbooks in my arms . . . all of it suddenly seemed ridiculous. Was that me?

—*You betcher skinny white ass that was us—we were amazing!*

"So this guy starts snogging me, right in the middle of the street, yeah!"

Susan's stories of the Edinburgh streets always seemed to be peopled with thieves, beggars, and gorgeous Scottish rapists.

Was that me?

The bar we frequented had a ledge with a mirror next to it to accommodate us standing-room-only types in the ladies' washroom. Was that me? Breathing in through one white nostril, then looking in the mirror sniffing, sniffing through the acrid drip of it down the throat. The girls, all laughing, all of us embracing: a group hug, a sort of group snort. Except I was the only one who felt like touching had just been invented as we all tore away and Susan pulled her gloved hand casually over the nape of my neck.

"You've got great hair, Giselle, only you should comb it," one of the girls said apologetically as someone began to pound on the door.

"Keep yer bleeding shorts on! It's open!" Susan yelled.

I stared at myself, noticing that my hair *had* become matted. How had that happened? I thought of Holly then. How, when we were kids, I'd make her up in front of Mom's vanity mirror, sprinkle sparkles on her eyes, smear wine-red lipstick on her cheeks, and she'd sit there patiently trying to hum while I transformed her into a child-whore.

"Greg likes you," head of the black-mini-dress girls whispered to me.

"Who?"

"Greg, the guy who was sitting on your left, next to Susan."

Susan let out another peal of swearing, and when the door banged open there were suddenly girls squealing all around us.

"Omawgawd! I have to pee sooo bad!"

Susan gave me a black look, which I ignored while rolling a twenty to sniff the last of the white powder off the ledge. There was quite a bit left over in all of our hugging and goofing around.

Then the girls left at once and I was alone. I went to the sink and cupped my hands under the faucet and scrubbed my face clean, like Holly had so many years ago, careful to get everything off like I told her to before our parents came home.

I looked at my red eyes and nose in the mirror. I considered my body, surely not attractive, surely not thin enough; it seemed to me all those girls were leaner, slinkier than me.

Suddenly I felt blood rushing to my head. I couldn't block out the thought of the blue innards of the cadaver we had opened that week, pickled in formaldehyde. Dead organs are a peculiar muted hue, and though I was skilled with the knife, I wasn't quite used to being inside a dead person, handling pale organs.

I can't remember what happened next except that when I woke up on the floor, my head and back ached.

When Susan found me I was still on the floor.

"Jaysus Christ, Giselle, is this why you don't drink?"

"I'm OK," I said, stepping up to the shaking floor, grinning at Susan.

"They said you had a seizure."

"Don't worry about Greg, Susan. I don't like boys. At least, I don't think I like them." I staggered into the door as it flew open and hit me square in the head. A golf-ball-sized bump formed almost immediately.

Was that me?

"Ow." I managed to look back once more at the mirror before Susan strong-armed me out.

The next morning I examined my bloodshot eyes and swore it would be my first and last cocaine experience. But when I looked into the bathroom mirror I saw more than the evidence of a wild night: a change had taken place. Someone else looked back at me grimly. I knew her skin barely covered the grotesque machinery of her squirming insides. Then she spoke her first sweet words to me:

—*You think those people like you? You think they're your friends? They're not your friends, they just feel sorry for you.*

She didn't speak much, not like she does now, but she

showed me things, images. The next day she forced my legs to walk faster everywhere I went and she screamed when I reached for another piece of bread.

—*Are you really going to put that in your mouth?*

When I gazed at her in the mirror, her judging feline-eyes reminded me that I was not good enough, that everything I had—school, body, and life—I had to maintain, work twice, three times as hard as everyone else to keep. She terrified me into spasms at night when her great pumping heart sucked all the excitement from my veins and turned it into criticism.

—*Do you think you're special? Because you have a head full of knots and facts?*

In those first quiet moments staring at her reflection I closed my eyes, willing her to disappear. But I could hear the sound of a knife cutting into her soft pale arms. I imagined her slicing us apart, just to show me our blood. That morning she was just a shell, still forming over my skin. But minutes later, when I looked back in the mirror, she had begun to take over; her deep wet eyes blinked back at me, alive.

—*Introduce me,* she yawned. *I want to meet your friends.*

A good surgeon knows biochemical pathways and anatomical landmarks intimately.

I measured and weighed her when they brought her home, counted her fingers and toes, and tested her reflexes. Unlike me, Holly was born long and skinny: nine pounds, nine ounces. She would not tolerate swaddling—her legs kicked at blankets, toys, and anyone who found themselves in her direct line of fire. Anyone except Dad. She wouldn't kick at him. She was considered slow because she wouldn't talk, although she learned to walk quickly. She moved drunkenly, falling a lot, but she was determined.

Holly had a funny habit of lying down on the ground and putting the right side of her head on the floor when she was sad or upset or tired. She'd suction her little pink ear to the wooden floor of our house, stick her thumb in her mouth, and stare at the dust beneath the furniture, meditating on whatever injustice or punishment she had just endured.

You couldn't touch her when she was on the floor; she'd thrash about and punch if you tried to pick her up. It was best just to leave her, to wait for Dad to cajole her out of her black mood.

Holly was born deaf in her left ear.

"I go 'way now" was Holly's first complete sentence. She said it to me, on the floor, squeezing out hot tears. Her shaky voice, her attempt at language, betrayed how very hard she was trying to be good. We were trying to get her to communicate, in those days, with monosyllabics. We'd cheer and dance around the kitchen, and sign back at her gleefully when she grunted an "uh-uh" or "na-huh." We were trying to break her of the habit of being silent for days and then waking up screaming.

"Holly good girl! Holly, you're talking!" Instinctively I reached down to touch her but she moaned and clenched the floor. She balled her fists into her face and wept bitterly. I withdrew my arm. Mom was cooking dinner, the pressure cooker was whistling, Dad was reciting poetry in the front room. It was altogether too much noise.

Born into a world of half words and blaring radios, of singing Hungarians and ongoing dramas, Holly went underground when our ever goddamn dynamic family got to be too much. Holly learned early on how to get us to disappear, or at least shut up, for a little while.

Me? I was born between the old world and the new, five months after my parents came to this country, and it's taken me twenty-two years to figure out how to get some control, some peace and quiet, and even now it's not so quiet.

# chapter 2

When Giselle came home for Christmas holidays last year I saw it happening. I saw her eyes dance across the food at dinner, calculating, making plans about how she could get rid of it. She had several tricks. One of her favourites was to take a couple of bites of her meal and then scrape the rest of her dinner into the garbage when she thought no one was looking. But she couldn't do this for too long, because I caught on early and told Mom.

When I heard it was a sickness, I went to the library to do some research. *The Perfectionists' Disorder. The Girl Who Thought She Had No Stomach.* I sat there, very still, with those books spread out on the clean, shiny table. I sat there in that quiet library with the tick of the clock in my ear, looking at those girls with big heads and awful long bones that looked like they hurt poking through the skin.

In late April, when Susan, Giselle's roommate, called us with news that Giselle was in bad shape, I chewed all the nails off one of my hands.

"She finished her year," Susan told me before I passed the phone to Mom.

"She's in the top ten and she wants to stay and do some summer courses but I think she needs help."

I wasn't surprised. Mom and Giselle's doctor arranged for her to go to the best clinic in the city straightaway, even though there was a mile-long waiting list. I'm not sure if Mom used Dad's title as a doctor to pull some strings, or if Giselle was so sick she needed immediate attention. Whatever the case, Giselle went to the clinic after a certain "episode" at school. Susan was never clear about what this "episode" was. Maybe Giselle passed out somewhere, or maybe she lost it completely and started chucking food at the other students one day in anatomy class. Anyway, school had had enough of her and she, it seems, had had enough, too. But I don't mean she was cooperative, because she wasn't.

"I have a test tomorrow!" she railed, gnashing her teeth at the clinic's receptionist. "I don't have *time* for this!"

"Shh, honey, don't worry about the test . . . you can make it up," Mom said, smoothing Giselle's hair back, massaging warmth into her arm with her fingers. Mom and I both tried to hold on to her and get her to lie down, and we both stared openly at the plastic medical band that hung off her tiny wrist, at the scratches and bruises on Giselle's arms and legs. It looked like she'd fallen off her bike or something.

"What happened?" Mom asked as Giselle plucked at her hair like a madwoman. For someone who was not eating enough, she was really hyper. She asked the nurse a stream of questions and she even had the nerve to put me in a headlock. I resisted the temptation to pinch what was left of the flesh on her bones and wriggled out of her hold.

"So long you morons!" she screamed as a male nurse wheeled her down the hall.

"She doesn't mean us, Mom, or anybody, she's just babbling, just talking."

I realized later she was either hyped on caffeine pills or

something stronger that went around school, or maybe she was just delirious. Mom said, "I hope they fix her hair."

Giselle's hair, which had always been neatly combed, long, and a gorgeous treacle colour, had transformed into a yellow nest of long dreadlocks that were tied back with a large hair elastic and a piece of fabric. I liked Giselle's new hair, although it was huge, and shrunk her face, and kind of made her look like a scarecrow.

"She seems high-strung, Ms. Vasco," the nurse said. "We're going to administer some sedatives."

"Fine," Mom told the nurse stiffly as she gripped my hand.

Mom had trouble recognizing the healthy-bodied, long-haired, upstanding daughter she had dropped off at the university not ten months ago, and maybe she hated, or at least feared, this wild, loud-mouthed, dreadlocked, sinewy creature posing as Giselle.

"Let's go," Mom said, her face darkening. "We'll come back tomorrow to see how she is."

I held up my finger, telling her one minute, one minute, and dashed down the corridor.

Giselle was propped up on the bed in a little hospital gown and the nurse was searching her arm for a vein. She seemed a lot calmer when she smiled at me.

"This is my sister. She's fourteen," she told the nurse, as if I were famous and she were very proud of me. The nurse nodded at me and continued to feel around in Giselle's arm, searching for the elusive vein.

"How's Mom?" she asked suddenly, very seriously, dropping her crazy-act.

"You've done a great job of flipping her out."

"Yeah, well . . ." She scratched her head, dislodging some of the neatly arranged dreadlocks from her ponytail, and then looked at me guiltily. She looked over at the nurse, who still had the needle hovering above her tiny arm.

"Give me that!" And in one swift motion, my sister pulled the tourniquet around her arm tighter, with her teeth, grabbed the needle from his hand, and injected it into her arm like an expert junkie.

"Don't worry," she said, pulling a silencing finger up to her lips, "I won't tell anyone. Besides, I'm a doctor." She laughed quietly, then closed her eyes, behaving as if the drug had had immediate effect. The nurse, who looked as if he wanted to punch Giselle in the face, pulled the needle out of her hand and snapped the tourniquet off. He was muttering something about spoiled university hotheads as he left the room. Giselle opened her eyes really wide then.

"Do you ever get hungry?" she asked. "Too hungry to eat?"

. . .

Six weeks later, after Giselle stopped acting so crazy, the doctors and nutritionists at the clinic were so impressed with my sister's progress—she seemed eager to "heal herself" and within the month and a half gained back almost half the weight she had lost—that they said it was OK if she came home early.

But now that she's home and "healing," Giselle seems different. Even though the clinic taught her about nutrition and stuff, she's gotten really weird about food. I don't know what she picked up in there, but she cuts it up into tiny pieces and eats really slowly, chewing every little bite about thirty times and moving her plate around in circles to examine it from different angles. But she has no problem eating crap. And knowing Giselle's weakness for sweets, Mom's stocked the fridge and shelves with all kinds of cookies, cake, ice cream, and chocolate.

Today she sat down next to me at the table with a tub of ice cream, which she scooped out with an Oreo cookie and licked off.

"You shouldn't eat that shit," I told her. It's so annoying that she acts like a baby, doing anything she wants because she's "sick." Her hair is only getting bigger and rattier-looking and she hangs out in her pyjamas all day. Plus, her skin is looking bad from all that sugar.

"I," she said, pausing for effect, and to grind the cookie with her teeth, "I can eat whatever I want. Doctor's orders." She grinned at me with black cookie stuck between her teeth. As I got up to take my plate to the sink, she started scooping out the ice cream with her finger.

"Besides," she added, scratching her back, "I don't eat it, it eats me. Want some?" She held out her spindly little finger and giggled. I slammed my plate in the sink.

I hate watching her sit around all day on the couch, too tired from her sugar highs to do anything except stare at the TV. She talks about going back to school, but it's hard to imagine her pulling herself together to even leave the house. How is she going to be a normal person and go back to school while she still looks like a scarecrow and eats crap? So I decided to do something about it: I got a garbage bag from under the sink and started throwing all her junk food into it. Then I walked over to her and snatched the tub of ice cream from her hand.

"Hey!" she whined, tripping out of her chair. "What the hell are you doing?"

"Until you eat and act like a normal person I am absconding with your food."

"Absconding?"

"Yes, absconding."

"That's a mighty big word, Holly. I didn't know they taught those kinds of words in grade six."

"If you cared about anyone other than yourself, you'd know I was in grade eight."

"Snot."

"Bitch."

"You can't talk to me like that!" she shrieked. Giselle was standing up now, swaying like a paper-ghost in her thin pyjamas.

"Why? Because you're sick? Because you act like a spoiled brat? Well, guess what, Giselle, I'm not your therapist and I'm not your doctor. I'm not Mom and I'm sick of your whining and I *can* talk to you however I want. I'm your sister and I know you and don't care if they tell you that you can eat whatever you want. You can't. You want to act like a baby? Then I'll treat you like one. You can do whatever you want in front of Mom or the doctors but not me. Understand?"

All of this shot out of my mouth in tears and spit as I stood there shaking my twenty-two-year-old pimply sister, who looked younger than me, who, I, at fourteen, could've thrown across the room like a rag. I couldn't help myself. Dear God I'm sorry, but I couldn't help it: I wanted to hurt her.

"You don't understand," she whispered.

I'm bigger than Giselle, bigger arms, stronger legs, wider torso, but I was still afraid of her until that moment, until I felt my thumb hit the soft inner bone of her arm.

Then, instead of hitting her, I put my mouth up beside her ear.

"You are so goddamn right I don't understand. But then you are the smart one and I am the stupid one. What do you want, Giselle? More food? More ice cream? I want to give you your wish, Giselle . . ."

"Shut up!"

I gripped her arm, till it felt like it might snap, till she cried out in pain, till she somehow managed to wrangle herself from my hold and crumple down on the floor. She covered her face as if I had hit her and, as I looked down at my shaking hand, which still held the garbage bag, I saw the trail of black cookie saliva smeared up the side of my arm, and the red mark where Giselle had bit me and freed herself.

. . .

Tonight the house is a tense hot place with Giselle fuming in her room and slamming doors, and so I go for a run. Mom and Giselle don't know that I sneak through the back door and run through the park. At night I can't see the crooked paths, so they don't trouble me. When I reach my stride, when I am warm and a single flame burns inside my gut, when something in me feels like stopping, that's when the lines of trees blur quicker and I push on harder. I see nothing but my legs. The pounding of blood in my ears reminds me that my heart is always with me, like breathing or dying. Then my legs disappear and I forget about Giselle's scratchy hair and ugly frowns, forget that we're bound together in bone and blood in this big messy life. When I kick against spring-wet trees, leap gutters in time, I find my own heart, alone.

# chapter 3

The speed of a marathon runner is directly proportional to the heightened cardiac output.

When she's not running in my dreams, she's swimming, and Holly's body is always a small vessel I cannot save.

We are at steam baths, standing barefoot on a clean, tiled floor. Holly keeps hopping from foot to foot and yipping like a puppy till I yank on her hand to get her to stop. We are wearing only towels. Holly is much younger, maybe five.

In the dream it is always the same: an old woman with pendulous breasts weaves her way towards us. She grabs me by the hand and points to the red mark on my palm and asks me, in a foreign language, if I am menstruating. Annoyed, I tell her, in English, that I am not. I explain that the cashier stamped our hands when we paid to get in. In vain, I search for the word "ticket" in a language I do not know. "Where's her mark?" the woman demands as she snatches my hand away from Holly's.

"Leave us alone," I growl, trying to wrench myself from the woman's grasp.

Suddenly Holly leaps away from me and dives into the shallow bath. The woman and I watch her swim the length of the pool underwater. As the pressure of the old woman's dry hand intensifies I remember that Holly cannot swim.

*Do you ever think about how your sickness affects your family?*

I can see them. They sit like a family of bronzed dolls facing the lake, their backs tight and wiry, deep brown from the sun. Mom sits on the beach below, looking up from her magazine every once in a while to pull her hat down over her eyes. I am sitting under a tree, away from them, in the background, a pair of Mom's big Jackie O sunglasses resting on my cheeks. Holly is three; she and Dad are playing catch with a large plastic blue-and-green ball. Dad is careful not to throw it too close to the water, lest she be hauled into the lake that she fears with the passionate irrationality of a toddler. I have my sticks, an array of interesting bugs, a caterpillar or two, and, my most prized possession, a tiny fat tadpole stolen from the minnow trap in the stream nearby, caught early that same morning before anyone is up to tell me not to.

I am taping them all to pieces of cardboard and labelling them with their Latin names, which I locate in the heavy encyclopedia I have hauled down to the shore for this purpose. I am still not sure what to do with the fish, however.

"Oh, Giselle," my mother says before we go down, trying to stuff a snorkel into my bulging beach bag. "Leave the big book at the cottage."

I offer her a fern stem in response. "It's so perfect, Mama.

Look, look at the back, they're called spores, they come from outer space." She smiles and tucks the fern behind her ear, and takes a handle of the bag so that the encyclopedia can come, too.

It's so hot the tape is barely sticking to the cardboard. I shove my heels deep into the sand, seeking out the cool, dark earth beneath the white layers. I tug off the tape: it has pieces of bark and sand stuck to it. Messy, messy. I take a break, watching Holly and Dad instead. Every time she catches the ball—which is a lot for a little kid—she yells and kicks up her heel. Dad signs at her to throw it back to him, which she does, hard and off course. Laughing, he dives for her throw, falling into the lake, hamming it up so that she laughs even louder. Holly shrieks, kicking sand into the water. She walks to the shore to watch him swim out. I get up, brushing the sand from my bathing suit, and dive in after him. In an instant, all the buggy-grub and sweat is washed from my hands and body. I start to swim out to him, eager to show him all the new tricks I've learned throughout the school year at my weekly swimming classes. As I paddle, weaving towards him unsteadily, he sees me coming and starts swimming back to shore.

"What you doing?" he asks, splashing me, then spitting water out the side of his mouth, his voice thick and gurgled.

"Look, Daddy, I'm a mermaid." I dive under and twirl my legs in the air but I forget to cover my nose, so I come up coughing. Then I feel his hands on my ribs, lifting me out of the water, lifting me high, high, till I am floating above him looking down on the lake. Thinking this is a game, I screech like Holly and leap from his hands, but he clutches at my bathing-suit straps and smacks his other hand square in my face to break my dive. There's water in my lungs, burning. My face is burning as hot-red as my tiny aching lungs, though nothing can burn underwater.

"What are you doing?! I was jumping, Papa, jumping, like a dive, you know, stupid?"

I start to smack him back on his head. His black hair is pasted to his skull, his angular jaw set, the bones in it clicking. Hysterical, I scream bloody murder until his big hand closes down on my mouth, clamping my protests.

Then he tucks me under his side while I kick and scream. My mother catches me as he pushes me in the water like a too-big fish he doesn't want. I slide into her arms. He begins yelling in Hungarian, waving his hands, smacking at the water. My mother says nothing except, "It's OK, Gizzy, I got you now." Then another barrage of sound back at my father that ends with English words: "swimming lessons."

He turns his back on us and crosses his arms, his chin falling to his dark brown chest. Holly steps on his feet, pokes him in the stomach playfully, her sign language for: "You OK?"

He pulls her up by the arms, comforting her. A quick look of terror, of guilt, passes between my parents. Then Mom wraps me in a big orange towel and asks me if I want something to eat. I shake my head, cough extra-loud so that he can hear it. But he doesn't, because he's halfway down the beach, clucking nonsense softly into Holly's bad ear.

Do you ever think about how your family affects your sickness?

That same night Holly's hip is glued to mine while I'm reading about crickets under the covers with my flashlight and worrying about the tadpole that I haven't had the guts to take out of the yogourt container yet, who is still under my bed growing fatter. Holly's sleeping with her mouth open, emitting baby-sighs every now and then. Her hand is tucked into the small of my back, sweaty and hot, but necessary; Holly can only fall asleep when someone is touching her.

I hear him get up to use the bathroom and snap off the flashlight. He hasn't said a word to me all day except, "Gizella, take out your wet towels. Hang up them." I strain my neck to hear his footsteps as he comes back down the hallway towards my room. He pauses, then opens the door gently and comes to the edge of the bed.

I cinch my eyes shut and feel his arm brush mine as his hand reaches out to stroke her sleeping baby face, her hair, then my shoulder. I murmur. I feel his ice-blue eyes on me. They evaluate, they judge, these feline aqua eyes. They can see me even in the darkest room in the cottage.

He eases the flashlight out of my hand. I grip it for a second, then give it up, pushing my head deeper into the pillow, still feeling those clear-water eyes on me. I pout my lips, like Holly does when she wants a kiss from him, but this trick never works with me. Instead, I feel her hands push against the base of my skull. She lets out another baby-sigh into my neck and her warm sweet breath swarms around me, forming a ring that guards me from whatever score he has come to settle. He retreats, but not before my own eyes fly open and meet his.

He blinks twice, his judgment, for once, suspended. He is curious about something. What?

I can see every eyelash, as if under a microscope, thick and teeming with life. Like mine, his eyes appear blue but are transparent. He blinks again, in amazement, seeing them, twin blue circles staring back at him, now, for once, without malevolence, without coquettishness. Could it be a truce?

He stands there for a while, his eyes glowing with so many questions.

*Where did you come from?* his eyes telegraph through the darkness.

*And when, when are you going to leave?*

*It is natural to wonder, at some juncture of your medical studies, whether medicine is really the human profession for which you had hoped.*

It may seem as if I'm indifferent to my family. Holly makes the case with her huffing and puffing and fighting, she makes the point that I virtually destroyed us with my breakdown. I'm not indifferent. I know I hurt Mom with it, I see it tugging at her eyes when I leave a half-eaten plate of eggs on the counter, when she collects my clothes from the laundry basket and sees I'm still wearing the same holey T-shirts I had when I was fifteen. She would like it if I were bigger, stronger, less prone to colds and hacking coughs. She would like it if I were like other girls and bought new clothes all the time, gained a few extra pounds, for padding, for when I might need another layer between myself and the world. I feel bad for Mom, but I can never tell her, or Holly, that he started it.

He started the whole mess with those ice-blue eyes that kept me begging for my right to exist. Holly doesn't know what it's like to love someone who doesn't care whether you live or die. She doesn't yet realize that love unreturned eventually transforms into a fierce tangled mess, nerves and entrails exposed like split animal innards. She doesn't understand that sometimes the unrequited must demand reparations, that love can be a mean and spiteful process, that sometimes one loses patience with love. So, when the nerves and guts have seemingly been packed away, sewn in and cleaned up so as not to make all the innocent bystanders uncomfortable, the carrier of this love becomes heavy with a toxic lump that grows, slowly and steadily, into a fierce ball of scarred tissue.

Located two ribs below the heart, it is called hate.

# chapter 4

Giselle doesn't talk to me for days after our fight but that's OK because I've been mostly at the track after school and don't see her much anyway. Our stupid fight becomes buried under silence, and the clacking of morning-coffee spoons in cups.

But yesterday, after a week of moping around in her pyjamas and lying on the couch staring at the TV, Giselle ate breakfast with us. She's even started talking about going back to school and volunteering at the hospital with Mom. She also got dressed and drove herself to her group meeting.

And maybe, just maybe, the old Giselle is coming back.

Today she was considering her hair in the mirror, trying to tame it. I saw a change in the corners of her hot-pink cat-mouth, which has been drawn and grim since she got back from the clinic.

"What?" she demands, all grouchy, when I stick my head into her room.

"I'm sorry." I stand in her doorway as she sorts our laundry. Giselle looks up, a stray blond braid falling over her face. She's flushed, a little tanned, almost healthy-looking. She licks her lips and hands me a pair of shiny red shorts.

"You'll need these to win." My lucky red shorts, worn only for races.

"Thanks." I step over the basket and pull her to me.

"Wha . . . ?" Giselle stumbles as I pull her into a hug. Her hips pierce my side. I put my hand on the small of her back and feel the knobs of her spine coming through her shirt.

"I'm sorry," I say.

"Why? What have you done?"

"Nothing." I hold on to her for a second too long, till she pulls away from me and I smell something like summer in her hair.

. . .

Ever since she was little, Giselle always wanted to be a doctor, like Dad. She's got the science gene. The one that's missing in me.

Giselle used to give the neighbourhood boys a dollar for squirrels. Fifty cents for birds. She made them promise not to hurt them and told them only to bring her roadkill, but I know they used to shoot them with BB-guns, because Giselle spent a lot of time taking bullets out of sparrows' chests. She used old scissors, tweezers, pliers, and salad tongs especially for this task.

One time, she stole some of our dad's special scissors from his travelling medical kit, and when he found out, his face went all red and he yelled at her.

"I told you not to touch my stuff!" he snarled, crossing his eyebrows, as he often did at Giselle, and yanking a stethoscope out of her hand.

I'd crouch over the animal as she operated, and to this day

the smell of latex and hospitals reminds me of Giselle because she made me scrub and wear plastic gloves.

I'd pick flowers for the grave and we'd bury the animals in the back of the garden and have a little ceremony. She took her time stitching up the wounds in neat little grids that reminded me of the scars on Frankenstein's neck.

"Come here, come closer," she'd say when she finished pinning the folds of the skin back. "Look, see it? See the heart?"

. . .

When our father had a heart attack, I sat, for what felt like a very long time, on the stairs, listening to my mother speak into the phone. She said our address in a quiet voice. She spelled out our last name slowly, as if she were reading the letters for the first time.

"Vasco," she'd said. "V-A-S-C—like cat—O."

Then she put the phone down gently and stood there, her whole body trembling.

I ran up the stairs and into Giselle's room and found her under the covers. She was shaking and sweating and crying on her pillow. "Giselle," I said. "Giselle, he is dead." Then she grabbed me up into her arms and there was nothing inside me.

She was holding me so tight, as if I were him, and not yet dead. As if all her life and tears could fill me up and I could become him again. So I said he was dead over and over in her ear until it sounded like a scream while she held me like that. So that she would know that it was me and that he was allofa-sudden dead.

# chapter 5

For each minute the heart is stopped, it loses a high percentage of capacity to perform muscular activity and becomes weakened.

Heart lesson #1: first meeting. Remember to keep breathing.

I was standing outside the entrance of the hospital, and I'd just bummed a cigarette from a patient after my group meeting, when I saw a sheepish-looking boy with a broken wrist and long curly hair spilling down his back. His look caught me off guard, sent shivers to my gut. He was fumbling through his pockets with his good hand, searching for matches. When he finally noticed me, he looked startled. He took a step back and put his hand on the wall to steady himself. His eyes stripped me, but for some reason this didn't make me uncomfortable like it usually did; it seemed familiar, as if I had just stepped out of a bath and he was waiting, with a towel in his hands. My hands started to shake. His look seemed to be reaching for something that was knotted in me, and the feeling of undoing the bind was somehow painful. Then I realized: I knew him.

I avoided his gaze, looking instead at the traffic, trying to figure out where I had seen those bedroom eyes before. He continued to look, so I, not being one to turn down a dare, gawked back. We ended up staring at each other for a good five minutes, while leaves whipped around in small circles, while I shivered in my clothes and he ran his hand through his dirty curls. We challenged each other silently. I think I may have sighed with relief or frustration when he started walking towards me.

"Got a light?"

"Yeah." I offered him a single washed-up match and a ball of lint.

"Thanks. You a doctor?"

"No."

"Well, can you take a look at my wrist?"

I wondered then if he knew we were at a mental hospital and not the walk-in.

"I'm not a doctor, I told you. I think you're confused, there's a walk-in just across the street . . . it's right—"

"I know you."

"Yeah?" I asked, curious, despite myself.

"Yeah, you used to hang with Joanne Marinelli."

"Sort of." I wrapped my arms around my chest and hopped from foot to foot to keep warm, taking sharp drags of my cigarette.

"Yeah, I played hockey with her brother, her brothers. You have a younger sister, right? She's, like, a kick-ass junior track star?"

I nodded.

"Yeah, I remember you. You used to come to those games sometimes with Joanne, and you guys would—"

"OK, stop now, that's enough."

He lit his cigarette and tugged at his ear, giving me a ridiculously beautiful smile, all teeth. Then I knew exactly who he was.

"And you are . . . Sol, right? Your hair's so long now."

He nodded, looking a little pleased.

"Your dad is some celebrity too. He writes for the *Sun*. He used to write about your hockey games."

Sol's smile disappeared. He looked down at his torn cowboy boots. No one wore cowboy boots anymore, so why was I standing there thinking that they looked so great on him? That they were the coolest boots I'd ever seen? And why, why did he look like I had just hit him square in the gut?

"Sorry, did I say something wrong?"

Sol shook his head and then, looking straight into the grey sky, said, "I'm Simon Bohan's kid, yeah," as if he were admitting defeat.

He stuck his hand out and there was a sudden jolt of energy between us as I took it.

"Solomon, son of Simon," he said, offering up his smile again.

"Giselle, sister of Sports Star Holly."

"Giselle," he said, letting my name fill the air between us, "lover of hockey, and Purple Jesus Gatorade in grade nine."

"Solomon, the undefeated Sunny Valley defenceman."

I remembered watching Sol on the ice in my first year of high school, waiting to catch a glimpse of him after the game when he came out of the change room with his wet hair plastered to his forehead. He was one of the only boys my age I could stomach, who I almost liked. I remembered, one time, while we were waiting for Joanne's brothers in the minivan, asking Joanne why Sol never came to our dances and parties. She said something like: number one, Sol was of the Jewish Persuasion; two, he went to some hippie downtown school where everyone sat around smoking dope all day and studying Buddhism; and three, didn't I think I had hogged the Purple Jesus Gatorade long enough?

What no one ever tells you about love at first sight, or lust, or whatever the hell it is, is that it's infuriating. At that moment, standing there in the cold entrance of the hospital, I had the impulse to hit Solomon, hard and fast in the face. I resisted this urge, thinking I would go insane either way, were he to stay or leave.

"Can I buy you a coffee?" he asked. It took me a couple of seconds to refocus.

"Sure, but what about your wrist?"

"What about it?" Sol said, tucking his bad arm into his jacket.

"Shouldn't you have it looked at?"

"It's already broken."

. . .

In the café, I forget myself and share three chocolate chip cookies with Sol as we laugh about hockey and the Marinellis' yellow-and-brown seventies rec room.

"So," he says in a lull, downing the rest of his black espresso. "I heard a rumour you were in the hospital or something."

My smile suddenly feels like a death mask. I grin at him till my teeth hurt. Then, a flash: *her* face in the window, reflected back at us. How could I forget her? That I bring her with me everywhere?

Her face is wrapped under sheets of gauze. Her eyes are rolled back into her head, mouth frozen in a laugh. The strands of her hair, like liquorice-strap electrodes, are flung out dangerously; they threaten to attach themselves to Sol's skull. She's readying herself to sink her teeth into him and tap the fluid from his brain.

"What is it, Giselle?" he asks, touching my hand. "I'm sorry, was I not supposed to bring that subject up?"

"No, it's nothing, it's just that . . . How did you hear? What have people been saying?"

—*Everybody knows. Everybody knows what a weak and selfish person you are.*

"Nothing, nothing bad, Giselle. You know it's a small neighbourhood and a big family. I heard it through Joanne's brother. Really, I'm sorry, I didn't want to upset you . . ."

—*Show him.*

—No.

"It's been nice catching up with you." I get up out of my chair, put my coat over my arm, keeping my eye on her reflection. If I move fast enough she may not sink her tentacles into him. She may not poison him.

—*It's for your own good. I don't want you to be loved only when you are beautiful.*

"I also heard that you were in med school, that you were at the top of the class and everything," Sol says, reaching his arm across to me, his voice getting desperate.

I look at his arm as if it is some sort of dirty animal tail—it hangs in the air between us, over the table for a second, then falls back to his side. I press my lips together, feel the oil from the cookies coating my lips as I try to produce one of those famous smiles Sol and I have been dazzling each other with for the past two hours. Apparently I fail miserably.

"Giselle, I'm sorry."

"Why? There's nothing to be sorry about, *I'm* sorry. I'm . . ."

—*Sick. You're going to be sick. You're going to march out of this café, head round the corner to the nearest alleyway and make yourself sick.*

—Two cookies, actually one and a half only, he made me eat a whole one, you saw him. I'm better. It's OK. It's just a cookie. I can eat as many cookies as I . . .

"Sunny Valley Arena, early Saturday afternoon, final

playoffs. Rangers are down three to five against Burlingville. Burlingville, for Christ's sake. Their offence is coming on strong. Little Jew-boy, right here, is not feeling so great after his best friend Barney's bar mitzvah the night before, a little too much sweet wine, if you know what I mean. So there's this big corn-fed Aryan forward comin' down the blue line at me. Feels like every time I adjust my helmet, he's in my face, ready to knock me on my ass, but something tells me I can't let him in. Can't let him through. Do you know what it was?"

"What *what* was?"

She's retreated now. Sol's throaty voice frightens her.

"A pair of blue mittens waving, waving at me from the stands."

"I have blue mittens," I say stupidly.

Sol fixes his eyes on me, willing me to stay there, in the middle of that bustling café, with people bumping into us and giving us dirty looks, and the girl in the milk-splattered apron behind the counter screaming that she could make the finest allongé in the world if everyone would just stop rushing her. Everything stops.

"I mean I *had* blue mittens. I don't have them anymore."

Sol nods, comes around the table, and threads a finger through my belt loop. He grips it and then pulls me towards him. He smells like strong coffee, smoke, and soap. A small gesture, yet infinitely sensual, the feeling of his finger on the leather of my belt as he pulls my coat onto my shoulders.

"What happened, blue-mittens? Some big freak knock you down?"

"Something like that," I mumble, my hands shaking from too much coffee and him so close to me.

—*How long, do you think, before he finds out? Before you show him? Show him what you really are.*

# chapter 6

My best friend is Jen Marinelli and sometimes Giselle, but Giselle doesn't count. I wear my school uniform above the knee, just like Jen. Giselle gave me her skirt and kilt pin when she graduated and I like the weight of her pin there, above my left knee.

Jen likes Peter, a tall, shy Polish kid with pimples on his chin, and I like Marco. Marco's Italian, of course, but the problem is he likes my friend Kat, who, two years ago, in sixth grade, was the first girl to get a bra and her period.

There's something mysterious about Katrina, besides her big boobs and the open watery look of her eyes. Mr. Saleri has her starting on the volleyball team and she's second string on the basketball team. Kat plays defence, which is a good position for her because she doesn't move very fast and is tough to get through. Kat will play sports but isn't so crazy about gym. Jen and I love it. Today Saleri lets me and Jen play pick-up with the guys while the rest of the girls do gymnastics on the blue mats. Kat doesn't feel like playing today, so she makes some excuse about her period and Saleri lets her sit on the bench, but when we start playing she miraculously recovers and starts yelling. One thing about Kat is that she can scream. As soon as Jen or I get the ball, Kat starts in. I think even Jen, who thinks Kat is kind of a loser, likes it. It's nice having a cheering squad when sometimes you feel like no one passes you the ball.

When I get to take off my uniform, change into my gym clothes and sweat, and press my body up against Marco's, when I snatch the ball from his hands and send it sailing down the court, I feel like I can breathe again. Like I am outside running and dreaming and I am almost free.

For some stupid reason, after gym, I can't stop thinking about Marco for the rest of the afternoon, about how he always looks like he's tanned, and is one of the only boys who is taller than me. I write his name in the margins of my notebook during biology class, making the "a's" all fancy and making the looping "o" at the end of it big and perfectly round. I even think about telling Jen that I like him.

I can still feel his body mashed up against mine when I take my seat in history class. I wonder about how I could get him to start paying attention to me because I do see him around a lot. Sometimes the boys' basketball practices overlap with the girls' and I can arrange it, if there's a boys' game and a girls' game at the same time, so that I can sit on the school bus with him. I think about track and cross-country practice and how I could try to run with him, even though he is a sprinter and I run distance. I make a list of my good points, reasons that he should go out with me:

1. nice
2. not obnoxious like Jen
3. athletic (we'd have a lot to talk about)
4. good in English and history (OK, history, sometimes)
5. interested in French-kissing, holding hands and running my hands through his black, Italian hair, interested in meeting

his parents, going over to his house and watching TV, maybe going skating with him sometime.

As I'm drawing black lines over this information, Kat walks in late to class and takes the seat I've saved for her in front of me. I watch her golden crucifix bounce between her large breasts and understand that Marco won't ever notice me after he's noticed Kat. I look down at my own almost flat chest and scribble a note to her.

—*Kat: Do you like Marco? Are you coming to the meet tonight?*

—*1. Maybe 2. Yes,* comes her prompt reply, in her funny Polish handwriting that looks like Mom's.

*P.S. Please D. T. N.*

Destroy This Note. I crumple it into my pocket and lean over to inspect Kat's intent, angelic expression. I touch her layered blond hair, so lightly she doesn't notice, and I forgive Kat, a little bit, for taking Marco away from me.

# chapter 7

For open heart surgery, the sternum is divided longitudinally in the mid-line and the pericardial cavity is opened to display the heart and major vessels.

Heart lesson #2: incisions and loss.

Eve was my first and only major relationship before Sol. Like Sol, who cringes sometimes when I talk about guy friends from school, Eve had the gift of drawing me in with her brooding. Eve and I were together for three months, inseparable, before she left for Germany and I went to med school. It may sound weird, but Sol reminds me of Eve, at least on the surface; both are dark-skinned, serious, moody people. Also, like Sol, I had to keep a close eye on my Eve, who had a tendency to sulk when I flirted. Thinking about sleeping with Sol for the first time, I can't help but think of Eve for some reason.

The day Eve and I slept together for the first time, we had gone shopping at a chic downtown department store. She chose a ridiculously expensive pair of jodhpurs and shuttled me into the change room with her.

"Do you ride?" I asked when she ripped off her T-shirt and jeans. I could feel the saleslady's eyes burning a hole through the change-room door.

"No!" She laughed at my question.

"Then why? Shouldn't you keep the money for rent?"

"Don't you think I'm sexy?"

I did. The lines of the tight brown stirrup pants and the cut of the conservative jacket flattered Eve's waist. Although she dressed and acted like a punk, Eve was an aesthete and had an excellent sense of style; I should know, she loved dressing me up. I had never wanted money for myself, but suddenly I felt awful that I couldn't yet pay for the kind of clothes and things she needed. Before I could tell her how great she looked and how I was going to be a doctor and that, one day, I would be able to pay for whatever she wanted, she burst out of the change room and demanded a whip. Needless to say, the saleslady, a white-haired matronly type who looked as if she still took high tea, was less than helpful.

"The mannequin has a whip!" Eve yelled by way of being reasonable.

"The mannequin is for display purposes only, dear." Ms. Priss definitely had her finger on the security button by this time.

"How much?!" Eve yelled again, slapping the stitch of leather next to a display of orange suede shoes.

Then a miraculous thing happened, as it often did when I was in Eve's company: the saleslady conceded to Eve's whim.

"Tell you what, dear, that whip is complimentary. Consider it a gift with your purchase. Now, will that be charge or cash?"

"Charge," she said, blinking her eyes only once to register

her surprise and producing her credit card from her wrinkled old jean jacket. I picked up her discarded clothes from the floor of the change room and, half out of curiosity and half in order to avoid the saleslady's gaze, watched Eve sign the receipt in her tall, shaky, proud handwriting. But I had nothing to worry about. The saleslady was classy, she wanted no trouble, only another satisfied customer. Despite Eve's performance, she treated us respectfully and I liked that, and, although Eve acted like it didn't mean anything, I knew she did, too.

"Will you be wearing your purchase home? A bag for your clothes?"

"Yes, thank you." Eve tossed her head back, an old nervous habit of hers from when she used to have long hair. She pointed her small arched nose into the air, and when the card cleared, we left smiling and picking through clothes on racks as if we were rich girls.

Maybe it was the saleslady who gave me the confidence to do what I did later, back at Eve's studio apartment, with the industrial door bolted, as the crack of her brand-new whip sounded off her paintings. Maybe it was the cheap Argentinian wine we drank that night, the three bottles of it. Maybe, with the warm South American wine running through my veins, I could finally make my move. Maybe it was simply that Eve did look fantastic in those clothes: regal, commanding. Maybe it was Eve's long-haired German shepherds, Vengeance and Irony, who bounded around us eagerly, tripping into splotches of red and yellow paint as we ran through the studio, drunk and feverish with our own stupidity.

Maybe all first times are laced with that same tenacious anxiety and longing. Whatever it was, I wanted to be sure she wasn't just part of some strange fantasy I was having about being happy with someone. I wanted to clear it in my head, I wanted proof that I was alive and with her.

Eve finally collapsed on the couch to sip more wine. The dogs, exhausted, flopped down on the floor across from us and eyed us warily. I sat next to her and put my hand on the sleek taut material on her knee. She lay back as I pulled my hand up her thigh and let it rest casually between her legs. She angled her flushed face towards mine for a kiss that would last ten minutes, or three months, depending on how you looked at it. Before long, my jeans and all Eve's new clothes were lying in a pile on the floor. Something hot and troubled, like swarming bees, beat itself on the walls of my pelvis when she touched my body.

Whatever my inspiration, it wasn't until the night sky had shifted from black to dark blue that we fell asleep, our fingers and legs stretched across the canvas of her bed, our torsos wound together.

· · ·

It's a cloudy June day and I show up early to pick up Holly from the track. It's going to rain, so I sit in the car for a while watching her jog around as Saleri times her laps. Saleri is Holly's stocky, moustached, Italian coach, and there's something about him that makes you want to throw your arms around him and give him a big bear hug. He yells at her to quicken her turnover.

Holly keeps running around the track unflaggingly. I lose count of how many times she circles. I can see her breath in the early-morning mist. She is the colour of a colt and her legs swing out from under her loosely. The peaks of her shoulder blades stick out from under her tank top, and are somehow startling under the dim, overcast sky. They resemble brown boomerang-shaped stones skipping on water: now there, now buried in the smoothness of her back.

She is tall and long, like our father was. She has even inherited his monkey arms and the wide span of his hands, which accounts for her incredible control over a basketball. Like most show-offs, she prefers to take three-pointers rather than passing or doing a layup, and, while Saleri always gives her shit for this, ninety percent of the time the ball ends up in the basket. She stops running finally, walks with her hands on her hips to the centre of the field, kicks off her runners, and collapses on the grass. I get out of the car, crawl through the hole in the fence and walk over the track to her. I stand above her making faces until she glances at me and smiles.

"Hi, Gizzy." I hand her an apple and she shines it on her wet shorts and hooks her ankle over her knee, rubbing the arch of her foot. With her hair cut so short, and her face flushed, she almost looks like a boy. I think she has decided to survive adolescence by sweating her way through it. She squints up at the grey clouds swarming above us.

"We're picking up my new friend, Sol," I say as she munches the apple. Holly wrinkles her nose, as if she's eaten a brown part of the apple.

"Sol?"

"Yes, Sol. That's his name. He's a new-old friend, actually," I say a little too quickly. Holly shrugs with the apple clutched in her mouth like a pig, as if she doesn't care what his name is.

"Which group you going to? Agnes's or yours?" she asks, spitting the bad part out.

"Mine, but I think Agnes might come."

She sprints over to Saleri and grabs her sweatpants from the ground. He nods and waves at me. I shiver though it is a warm rain that has begun to fall.

When we get in the car, Holly starts playing with the radio. Halfway down the block to Sol's place, she pulls her fingers through her hair and squints at herself in the mirror.

"Do I smell?" she asks.

"You always do, brat," I say, tossing her a sweater to cover herself. I honk and Sol runs out of his house. I can tell by the line in his mouth that he has been waiting for me, that he is slightly annoyed that I am not alone, but this falls away when he opens the door and looks into Holly's shiny face.

He gives her his all-teeth Diamond Sol smile and something in my heart tightens. "I've heard a lot about you." His dark eyes take her in, in that unconscious sweeping way men have when they find a girl attractive. Then he looks at me.

"She's gorgeous, just like you said, G."

Holly starts giggling, almost choking on her apple core. Her face is turning redder.

"And fast!" she says, blowing apple chunks onto the window.

"And fast," I repeat, putting the car into drive.

. . .

When I get to the hospital, it turns out that group is going to be a spicy double-dose psychiatric special: I have to bring Agnes along to my meeting because there's been some kind of mix-up and the nurses want her off the floor for at least a couple of hours. Mom's a nurse at the downtown mental hospital and I just started working there, as a paid companion, it's called. I'd wanted to work at a lab instead, but then Mom got me this job, so I work with Agnes, mostly.

Agnes is a seventy-year-old schizophrenic woman from Penetanguishene. She likes the little sandwiches and cookies at the meetings and, because all the girls have eating disorders, she can have as many as she wants. I have to smuggle Agnes's coffee in under my coat, though, because coffee's not allowed. No gum, no cigarettes, no caffeine—it's like the total opposite of an AA meeting.

I sit between Agnes and Nancy, a middle-aged bulimic and self-appointed leader of the group. I think Nancy's kind of mad at me today because I was released from the hospital.

"The doctors are letting me go early," I'd said to her when I signed the release papers at reception.

"Oh, doctors, they think they know everything," she'd snapped.

I have mixed feelings about Nancy's tough-love approach, but I'm not really intimidated by her, or I try not to be. She comes off like a bitch but, after what I've been through lately, few people scare me. Besides, I've been having good days. Although eating three meals a day still really freaks me out, I try to reason with myself that eating a tuna sandwich for lunch isn't the end of the world, that there are more important things to think about than how full or empty I feel. Of course, this line of reasoning isn't always successful and occasionally I just can't finish a plate of food, but *she* has been keeping her distance and, at the end of my now-busy days of studying and working, if I start thinking too much about everything I ate that day and get depressed about it, I call Sol and we sit and talk in the park near my house and he rolls down the hill on the wet almost-summer grass like a dog until I pull him up into my jacket and kiss his soft face.

Nancy crosses her arms and frowns as I lean back in my chair and pick at my nails, to show her I could care less about her oncoming interrogation.

"You want to start today, Giselle?" Nancy asks.

"Sure."

"Why don't you tell us what kind of steps you've been taking."

"Well, OK, let's see, I've been going to the library to do research, I work with Agnes here—everybody say hi to Agnes." The girls squeak out hellos and Agnes opens her mouth to reveal a half-chewed cheese sandwich and her loose dentures. Just as I'm about to convince the crowd that I'm the success story of the month, Agnes pipes, "She's got a beau," before stuffing another sandwich into her face. Nancy gets all red as she adjusts her chair to better verbally assault me.

"Shut up." I elbow Agnes.

"So, you've just got out of the clinic because you lost so much weight at school that you barely finished your year, and now you're *dating* someone?" Nancy asks.

"Yeah, well, I don't know if we're dating, exactly, he's more like an old friend." I put my hands on my knees and squeeze them tightly.

"Is this your idea of taking control? Another relationship?"

"Well, first of all, we've only been seeing each other for, like, a week or something and, second of all, the last time I checked the anorexic's guide to recovery there was no clause against dating someone." The other girls start to whisper and smile; Nancy shoots them a look of death.

"All I'm getting at, Giselle, is that, and you'll pardon the pun, you seem to have enough on your plate right now without a boyfriend. You have to get control of your life, your eating habits, in a positive way, without distractions."

"Point taken. Can someone else talk? I don't really feel like sharing this right now." Nancy glowers while Agnes clamps her hand to my arm and starts singing "Que Sera Sera" softly into my shoulder. I take her hand and she squeezes it a little too tightly and then yanks it away as if I grabbed her.

A new woman, whom I've never met before, a tired-looking lady wearing a classic brown business suit, leans in as the other girls fidget in their chairs. When she talks, her voice is the opposite of Nancy's. It's pleading, low and smooth.

"Giselle, are you committed to being healthy?"

"Yes," I whisper.

"What helped you? What makes you strong?"

"My sister, my mother, work, and friends, I have some friends."

"Can you do it for yourself now, not for anyone else but you?"

I didn't mean to hurt anyone by losing all this weight, except I wanted to see what would happen if I stopped eating. It was an experiment of sorts, made easy by the late nights at the library, coffee, cigarettes, and OK, I confess, maybe a little speed too, sometimes.

It comes easy to me, almost too easy. It always has. While other girls sweat and fret, exercise constantly and watch what they eat, I can drop five pounds simply by skipping dinner a couple of nights. Some people are naturals, like Holly with running; I'm naturally good at losing weight. All I have to do is forget to eat.

And I'd forget a lot, which is hard to do in a European household, with eating being one of the major social events in our house. Maybe because they'd been deprived, our parents offered us the best of everything Thomas's salary could afford: the best private schools, the finest music and dance teachers, and, last but not least, copious amounts of rich, nourishing Eastern European fare. But while I should've been grateful for this, I wasn't. Early on in school I began to have the vague realization that my parents had expectations of me, big ones. Though I wasn't the athlete Holly was, I was good at science, like Dad, and, despite the fact that I'd already skipped a grade, I entered an accelerated program in junior high, without cere-mony, after Dad died. Around this time I began to balk at the lavish lunches and dinners Mom prepared, and while Holly gulped down spoonfuls of whipped cream and pleaded for more, I felt the need to set myself apart from my family, to reject all the food that was so integral to our nightly ritual; it seemed excessive, strange suddenly.

Maybe all children of immigrants are conflicted. On the one hand they live in the reality of the new world, on the other hand they have to contend with the ghosts and the stories of the old that seem unimaginable. Oddly, my parents had never formally taught us Hungarian, and, by the time Holly was born, they spoke English almost all the time. But I'd already picked up a fair amount from early childhood, and though my mouth had forgotten how to form the words, I could understand the things my parents talked about: wars, revolution, communism, lack of food and clothing—it all seemed so foreign to me. Even more unimaginable was that by dressing nicely and being smart, I could somehow make up for all they had lost.

It feels awful to put this into words, because my parents hadn't pushed me, or Holly (definitely not Holly), not really, to be the perfect lady, the perfect anything; they only wanted what all parents wanted—for their children to be good, smart, and kind. Maybe they wanted a little more, like all parents, maybe they wanted their children to be special. Besides, I'd inherited Thomas's mind. I couldn't squander that. But I'd inherited something else too: their suffering, which had brought me to this place. Born between these worlds that waged war on my ragged little teenage body, I became a terrible, ungrateful child. I conceded only to working hard at school and bringing home good grades. The rest of it, my mom's carefully prepared food, the extracurricular lessons she expected me to take, the expensive feminine clothes she wanted me to wear, I shrugged off indifferently. I began to dress down, wearing ratty jeans and dirty T-shirts as soon as I could, and although I could see how disappointed Mom was by my fashion sense and attitude, and it made my heart hurt if I thought about it too much—what a shitty kid I was—I couldn't help it; rebelling was completely out of my control.

"You're such a beauty, Giselle. Why do you dress like a homeless person?" was my mother's mantra to me throughout high school. Since I didn't disappoint her academically, we'd reached some sort of silent agreement whereby I would bring home top marks and she wouldn't nag me about eating and clothes. I was also careful to remain skinny, but not too skinny, so that she wouldn't freak out and start making me eat. Besides, Mom had enough to contend with, what with losing Dad, getting Holly to do her homework, and doing her own job, so I slipped under the radar of her stress and grief. I finally became grateful—grateful that she left me alone.

Then there was sex, which was decidedly scary. I simply wanted to avoid it, all of it. In high school, my friend Joanne showed me her dad's Italian porno magazines: legs opened, hairy skin on skin and opening yourself, opening myself, *there,* seemed impossible, ridiculous. Was this what love was? If it was, I would never be capable of it, of performing an act so utterly animalistic, so completely out of control. It was confusing and disgusting to me. At the same time I felt inadequate. There were boys and girls I liked, that I could imagine, eventually, wanting to be naked with, but they never took notice of me. I knew I didn't deserve their attention, that I had let too much go: I was too tall, too awkward, my belly was too bloated, my arms too thick. It got so I couldn't harness my own growing appetite for their desire, but I *could* make my stomach flat, I could starve myself until I felt my flat hipbones protrude and I could place my thumbs into the indents at the top of my narrow pelvis. I learned to control my desire for people, for food. And this is how I discovered a new intimacy which required no one.

While I craved attention, I was terrified of letting someone else into my imperfect, hateful world. It was me, and only me, who could control my cravings; denying myself food was proof that I was stronger, better than most people. But I was lonely for touch. Still, my own stiff regimen of stripping myself to the core and forcing myself to turn away from those curious eyes made me feel proud, if alienated; I was trading my new-found power of flesh for something more trustworthy, something pure.

Naturally skinny, but not dangerously so, I trod the line between waif and child as I grew into a woman. And hunger became my salvation; after a while, hunger, my sexless, undemanding suitor, was my only constant friend.

Site of wound: Surgical incisions placed in the lines of least tissue are subject to minimal distraction and should heal promptly, leaving a fine scar. In the face, these lines run at angles to the direction of underlying muscles and form the mask of facial expression.

Below my eye, there are two almost invisible scars that remind me of my last days at school. They are all I have in the form of concrete proof. Those weeks before coming to the clinic return to me only in fragments, like the rare shell-shocked moments of lucidity after an accident. Reflexes failing, I have only pictures; I retain imprints of flying shards of bone, glass imploding in my face. I remember the unseasonable heat of those early-April days and lying in bed watching the fan. I remember my shirt soaked with sweat and, finally, the matted feathers floating around me like soft rain. I remember the last days with clarity though: I spent them studying for finals, and virtually living at the library.

Day after day, I watched a serious-looking Korean boy, Thuy, his name was, sitting at the desk in front of me, sighing over impossible hieroglyphic equations. Thuy and I always claimed the same spot in the library, at the same big desk under the fluorescent lights. We liked to spread our books and papers all over the table as if the sheer display of all the notes we had collected could secure us from the horribly uncertain fate of failure. The information piled up silently in our heads and the panic of a new chapter would cause one of us to abandon a highlighter, cough, or get up for a walk, while the other valiantly studied on, offering an empathetic nod. A forgotten key to the lexicon of the carotid artery, like a half-remembered square root, would cause a minor gasp or leg spasm. When I looked up at him, at his waxy, pulled face, Thuy's eyes curled at me in a kind of lonely smile. He liked to peer over into my books as I twirled my newly plaited hair (the dreads had gotten so out of control I had finally had my hair professionally done at a Caribbean hairdresser's).

Thuy and I became manic partners in our quest for knowledge, for justification of the expensive university education we felt our immigrant parents had squandered on us. We became soulmates during finals and, while trading strawberry liquorice for rice balls, I asked him about engineering. He told me his father was a veterinarian and then put out his hand and taught me how to say "friend" in Korean. *Chingu.*

I scribbled out English-composition papers for him when he complained he was flunking a rudimentary English class and he helped me with chemistry; it seemed a fair enough trade. I regret now that I didn't get Thuy's number; he was my only friend through that blurred time, besides Susan, and Greg, if you could count them as friends.

Towards the end of the semester, I became obsessed with the machinations of the human body, all the miracles that took place every day to sustain us, to keep us clothed in this meretricious skin. The nightmare of unravelling, of death, seemed to be everywhere and I thought if I could learn it, if I memorized the visceral cartography, I could be saved, somehow, from my own nightmare of looking into the mirror to see my disassembled face with the lines undrawn, separate. I was beginning to understand death, and that what moved us was our fear of it. It got so I could barely get a couple of hours of sleep at night. I began to have nightmares about operating in the bright lights of the theatre with slippery, oversized instruments falling out of my hands. The organs would be in the wrong places and my blade would slip in my sweaty grip, cutting into marrow.

One day I was home trying to find a belt to fit me before heading out the door to my nightly library date with Thuy. I was edgy and irritable from not sleeping and I was only eating one meal a day. Usually something light like soup and rice balls and candy was all I, or *she,* could handle. I realized then that I'd lost some weight, though I thought I looked relatively normal—still chubby in the face.

While I was trying to lace a hippie guitar strap into my jeans, the doorbell rang. It occurred to me then that I'd never had guests over: the only people who ever visited the apartment were Susan's friends, while Susan, of course, on her rare visits home, would let herself in with her key.

"Hello?" I answered the door, barefoot, and, standing there, almost seven feet of him, was Greg, the guy Susan had a crush on at the bar.

He was sandy-haired, broad-shouldered, and wearing a purple and yellow leather varsity jacket that was vaguely disgusting to me. His eyes travelled up and down me until he met my eyes, and I cinched my belt in place and tapped the door with my fingernail.

"Yes?"

"I'm supposed to meet Susan here. Can I come in?"

"Uh, sure." I opened the door slightly and he swept in.

Greg sat down on the couch and flipped on the television casually, as if he owned the place, his long limbs folded over themselves like the pink and blue origami cranes Thuy would place on my textbooks during his rare breaks from studying.

I was slightly disconcerted with the idea of a stranger in my home. I sat on the broken La-Z-Boy chair Susan and I had dragged home during one of our treasure hunts in the student ghetto Dumpsters.

What did people do? I thought, staring at Greg. Oh, right, they offered food.

"Want some crackers? I'm sorry, I don't have anything else to offer you."

"No thanks."

I hadn't been with a human being besides Thuy in so long I wondered what to do next, and so we did what normal adults do to pass the time in a stranger's company: we drank.

After three exquisite Caesars mixed by Greg, and an exhausting series of stories about his football injuries and his father's oil business in the States, I got up from the La-Z-Boy.

"OK, that's it for me," I said. "Good night."

"Wait a minute." He reached out and grabbed my arm and pulled me back down.

"I don't know where Susan is, it's late . . . she might have forgotten about your date and I have to get up—"

"That's OK, sit down. Here I've been blabbing about myself all night and I haven't asked a thing about you. Are you a dancer?"

"No." I was appalled by the sensation of his arm. It was the first time I'd been sexually drawn to someone without wanting to be. The feeling was complicated and nasty somehow. With Eve it had been uncompromising, complete. I'd wanted to lose myself in her, like a book or a film. But I wasn't even vaguely interested in Greg's life, which seemed infinitely boring to me. If anything, I wanted to keep myself intact, on guard. I thought this as his hand snaked into my lap and he kissed me, and then all the thinking stopped. As his warm and spicy college-boy lips massaged mine, I wondered what I had gotten myself into.

"I didn't come here to see Susan." He looked into my eyes balefully and I fell for it. I drew my fingers up the length of his neck. He leaned into them as if they trickled warm oil, and then it was as if we had always been lovers, as if we were used to these quick and easy transactions of touch and pull.

"You can kill a man by slicing one clean stroke in here." I pulled my fingers up his neck, over his carotid artery, his main vein.

"So show me," he said, leaning in for one more cut.

· · ·

Greg left the next morning after a breakfast of saltines, stale cheese, and some uninspired conversation. I washed out the salt-encrusted Caesar glasses and then vomited bright pink bits of food into the sink, realizing that for all Greg knew, I *was* a dancer, not someone who understood the complicated mass of networks and systems of the body, and this suited me just fine. I decided not to leave the apartment. Troublesome things like Greg's body, like my voracious appetite for it and french fries, were out there in the world. Besides, I had wasted valuable time by spending the evening with him and needed every second I could get for more studying. I thought about lovely, lonely Thuy and cringed, wondering what he would think about my escapade with an American varsity-football star.

—*You goddamn slut.*

But after a couple of hours I felt better and fried up some sardines and drank lemon water. When Susan came home three days later, it was still hot. She found me in my underwear and bra, wearing a pair of papier-mâché wings pasted with white feathers. I know it's absurd and I can't remember the logic of that outfit, what I had been thinking or feeling when I strapped on those wings that someone had abandoned in our hall closet after a costume party. I remember only that I hadn't been eating much and that I had begun to black out periodically. Perched on the edge of the window, I must have looked like some ancient pterodactyl hybrid creature to Susan, because she started when she came into the dark apartment and saw me smoking a cigarette in the windowsill. She stood there, arms crossed, in the dark room illuminated only by the orange street lamp. Somehow I realized that she knew all about Greg, about how wasted and low I felt about it all.

"Hot, eh?" I ventured.

"Yeah. What are you doing?"

"Oh, nothing . . . hanging out."

"I see that. When was the last time you ate, G.? Or slept?"

I took a long drag of my cigarette and stared at it in my hand—how had it gotten there? Had I lit it? How had I managed that? I suddenly felt dizzy. I fell off the edge and onto the hard radiator, taking a tablecloth and vase down with me. Then, like some disgraced, unskilled Cirque du Soleil dancer, I covered my semi-naked body with my hands, curled into a ball, and started crying when Susan came to my side.

"Stop moving," she barked. "You're covered with glass." Indeed, my face, hands, and legs were bleeding. My exoskeleton had failed me. It didn't matter what I ate or didn't eat, I still wasn't safe from the indignities of the body.

I was terrified suddenly, but not of Susan, who'd starting picking pieces of glass out of my elbows and hair. Susan could not know that any insults she hurled at me would pale in comparison to the abuse *she* could levy. I knew then that there was a great purge ahead; admonishments, elaborate systems of torture would be inflicted. *She* was screaming now, steadily, high-pitched.

—*Exhibitionist! Slut!*

The fall had cracked her mouth open and dislodged her raspy voice.

Susan unstrapped the wings from my back, took a blanket from the couch, wrapped me up in it, and dragged me to bed.

"You're pretty strung out, eh, kid?"

I looked at her.

"I'm sorry."

"It's OK, G. I forgive you," she said softly, patting my face down with a towel before going back to the living room to make a long phone call.

Fear rippled through me in waves, my body shook, I was almost incapacitated, almost. I clawed at the covers. I was in trouble, in deep, deep shit. I hadn't been in so much trouble with *her* since the week before, when I ate almost an entire layer of Pot of Gold chocolates at a wine-and-cheese party for the Humanities Department and she made me pace my bedroom all night to burn off all the calories. Yet there was a tiny part of me that was proud that I had defied her. I'd proved that I could chew the head off any man who came looking for me. I was a beast, a force to be reckoned with. I'd proved something. Random and careless as the incident with Greg was, I'd discovered that I had a will, something outside of the parameters that she had set. I whispered to myself, giggled maniacally, as I thrashed around in the covers. I didn't know it then, feeling only the immature joy of a child who discovers the word "no," sensing, for the first time, the surge of assertion, of ego, despite his mother's quick slap.

My unformed will, not yet a voice, would fail in the short term, my quick hospitalization evidence of this. But it was still there, like the words uttered in a dream, in the soft sliding sound of Greg's athletic legs twined with mine, in the sound of the curt wet slice I had made in the frontal lobe of a pickled head in anatomy class earlier that week. My will, my very own, was gathering strength and speed like the gentle breeze that would eventually break the early-April heat into a wild tornado wind and slap rain into houses and send people rushing to close their windows.

I slept for days, ruined, starved, empty of all thoughts. I watched the rain pour down the windows, unable to acknowledge her screams, the fact that I was officially at war with myself.

Areas of incised wounds are inspected daily for warning signs of infection.

—*So, you gonna go back to school?*

—Maybe, when I'm ready.

—*How many ways can you say "self-destruction"?*

As I was lying there, in the hospital, with a tube up my nose, and cuts on my face, *she* came to me and pressed her cheek into mine. I tried to explain to the nutritionist, whose slim hands and sad bovine eyes always put me to sleep instantly; to the other girls in the group, who came around to sulk and complain; to Holly, who didn't even bother to listen to my wild ravings and instead put on her Walkman and danced around the room doing disco moves. It didn't matter that they couldn't hear me because nothing ever came out, at least nothing that ever made sense:

*Meet me on the corner . . .*

*Meet me at the Copa . . .*

Nothing I wanted to say ever came out right, because *she* was still screaming so loud in my head.

—*What an unbelievable mess you've made. What a supreme fuck-up you are.*

I thought if a sound came out and I told them a she-devil had just possessed my soul they'd put me somewhere even worse than where I was.

Still, I longed for someone to reach inside me and pull her out by her hair, because she took the smallest things from me.

At first, just trying to get up on my elbows was a monumental production, never mind eating or talking. And until I learned how to back-talk, how to wheedle the tiny incision blade from her hands in order to get my way, she threatened and swore at me. And while my peers wondered if they should go to Kenya, or assist in a city lab, I lay in a dark corner of their hospital, sweating about how she might kill me in my sleep.

# chapter 8

I dream of racing the way some people dream of showing up to school in their underwear. A week or so before a race, I'll wake with the sheets sweat-soaked and knotted around my knees and Mom clucking her tongue as she tries to untangle me.

The dream changes. Sometimes I'm on the inside lane on the track, behind all the other runners, and no matter how hard or fast I run, the distance never gets shorter. Instead, I fall farther and farther back with each pumping stride. Or, I'm on the outside track, ahead of the other runners, believing in my false lead till the gun cracks and I can't move fast enough; my ankles buckle under, my bruised and scratched legs collapse into the other runner's lane. Once I dreamt a bird shat on me right as the starter called: "One . . . Two!" That time I woke up laughing.

Mr. Saleri and I agree that I am no sprinter, that it takes me too long to warm up. My forte, as he puts it, is endurance, not sudden speed. But I'd had the best time at our school for one lap around the track and so I was racing for St. Sebastian in the four hundred today.

Mom and Giselle showed up to the race. Because she's skinny, Giselle looked like all the fourteen-year-olds around her, but somehow like an old woman, too. She was wearing a funny green tennis visor with a pair of big movie-star sunglasses (none of her old clothes fit her anymore so she's wearing my old stuff).

But I was too nervous to really care about how crazy Giselle looked, even with Bobbie Carpi, a pimply, stocky shot putter, making stupid comments about how "hot" my sister was, like a model or something.

When the blank went off in the starter's gun, I had a perfect lead. I didn't jump the line, I didn't collapse into the adjacent lane, I didn't make any of the mistakes I'd dreamt of. Instead, my back leg shot out from under me and propelled me into a series of perfect long strides and I passed five girls in the first hundred metres. Then I glided into place, behind a dark ponytail, just as Mr. Saleri had told me to, and held tight until the last hundred-metre stretch. In the last thirty metres, I passed the dark-ponytailed girl and saw Lucy's back. Always ahead of me, Lucy's muscled back.

The strange thing is, I don't even mind that she won. I shook Lucy's wet hand and blew the sweat off my dripping nose and felt OK. There was still a lot of work to do on my body, on my time. Lucy was my marker: if she could do it I could do it, and I would continue to do it, despite the constant ache in my knees and back.

Maybe the reason I didn't care about losing was that, as I was running the last stretch, something distracted me from the finish line: I saw my father. He looked a little older than he was when he died and he was wearing shorts, flip-flops, and a backwards baseball hat. It was Dad, or Dad's ghost, I guess, a little paler, a little more bloated, but Thomas all the same. He had his hands cupped around his mouth and was yelling: "Go! Go!"

He appeared again as I approached the bleachers where Giselle and Mom were. He was standing behind them eating an ice cream sandwich, looking as if he was eavesdropping on their conversation. Of course, he disappeared by the time I got to Mom and Giselle.

The last time our paths crossed today we spoke. I was in the locker room packing my gym bag when he poked my arm in the annoying way he used to when he was alive.

"Holly." He still had his accent, saying my name like "holy."

"Hi, Daddy."

"Why's your sister wearing that goofy sun visor? Why she is so small? I'm thinking it's you at first."

"She's sick, Daddy."

"Sick?" He looked alarmed.

"Sick, like, you know, mentally." I twirled my finger around my head, thinking maybe ghosts couldn't hear so well, that they needed sign language.

"Oh." He looked really confused and I wondered if I should explain the last nine years of our lives. I also wondered, if he was dead, when did he get a beer gut?

"Great race, Holly."

"Thanks, Dad."

"No really, you hear me shouting?"

"I did."

He didn't hug me or touch me, which kind of surprised me—he was an affectionate man, after all, that much I remembered (plus, I was his favourite). He just shuffled away slowly, his flip-flops clapping against the soles of his feet as he righted his baseball cap.

It makes sense to me now that he didn't touch me, because I know how difficult it was for him to even come and talk to me. Maybe he was afraid that he'd scared me. Maybe he thought he'd make his other daughter mentally sick too if he kept visiting me and having little heart-to-hearts. Maybe he thought his family had enough problems without him wandering around in summer clothes and giving out hugs. I don't know.

I stuffed my hoody sweater and my sweaty clothes into my bag and ran out to the parking lot, where Mom and Giselle were waiting. I glanced in front of me and saw him, walking away from us. I looked at Mom and Giselle, who were giggling and waving, and I moved towards them, holding back the urge to run after him. Suddenly a funny thought jumped into my head: *I had called him and he'd come,* I thought, watching him dissolve into the green field and dandelion fluffs. Something told me if I did run after him, want him too much, he wouldn't come back again. Not a second time.

# chapter 9

Cardiovascular activity increases serotonin levels as well as the rate of blood pumped to muscles.

Holly runs twice a day in preparation for her next big race on Friday, and the rest of the time she's locked in her room, with Jen, laughing her head off. Holly complains that I am becoming more like Mom since I started working at the hospital.

"How?" I ask, disturbed.

"I don't know, you give me that look and use her voice sometimes."

Agnes has also been difficult lately. Today she started in about my hair. It seems, among the many things she hates about me, she hates my dreadlocks most.

"What are you? Black or something?" she quipped when she first saw me. "Can't you wash yer fuckin' hair?"

"I'm blond, Agnes. I'm white. It's just a hairstyle. They're clean, clean as they can be," I explained pointlessly.

"Nobody's white! Not when girls are boys and boys are girls and blond girls make their hair up like darkies. Nobody's nothin' then!"

I took her to a coffee shop. She was wearing two heavy men's watches and had pink lipstick smeared all over her teeth. When she told me that they put dope in the doughnuts, I laughed and said I hoped so. Nobody told me that you don't joke with Agnes. She swallowed a lit cigarette and fell off her chair. It's not getting-to-know-you time, Mom explained to me later.

After my shift with Agnes is over, I pick up Sol from the newspaper. He climbs into the car, his long lashes drooping, his eyes tired and sad. Sol's a journalist, like his dad, but has, like, an intern position or something. He works at the *Sun* and does research. He spends all day in his father's shadow, chasing other people's words and stories and then comes to me with his hands coated in newspaper ink, black streaks on his face, clutching three newspapers and bitching about ad space.

When he climbs into the car he kisses me. It's the first time he's done this and the soft flesh of his lips sends a shock wave through my system. Automatically, I put my knuckle on the motor that lies beneath his rib cage, in the pit before his stomach, to feel his energy course through the rest of him. He's warm and I want to feel him close to me, feed off his warmth. As soon as I start thinking about it too much, I pull my hand away from his stomach, which gets him breathing faster, and when our mouths get hot he turns away. He fixes his eyes on the road and wipes his mouth, as if he's just said something wrong, and ends up smearing more black ink across his lips.

We get to the track and enter the stadium. He grabs my hand and holds it, tracing the bones in my fingers. I see Holly stretching and doing jumping jacks in her running tights and sweatshirt—she's decided against the sassy red shorts. If she places in this race, she goes to track-and-field camp. On the other hand, if her team wins next week, she gets to go to basketball camp.

Sol buys one of those huge red, white, and blue rocket Popsicles. "Want something?" he asks, pulling a ten out of his jeans. I shake my head.

"Two Pogo-Sticks, please."

"Sol!"

"What?" He smiles, his delicate eyebrows piqued. "Come on, you're Eastern European . . . What've you got against breaded stick-meat? Eat one, Giselle, I'll have the other." A little teenage girl with about eleven ear piercings hands him the food.

—*This is a test. You are being tested.*

—By a Pogo-Stick?

I pluck at my hair, desperate not to show Sol that the idea of eating a goddamn Pogo-Stick is enough to set me off. I feel ridiculous about the panicky state I'm in, then I remember when I was in the clinic how the nutritionist took us to a doughnut shop and made us eat doughnuts to show us that it was OK to eat food frivolously. That it was OK to eat when you weren't hungry sometimes, that that's what normal people did and it didn't mean you were going to get as big as a house.

I chew at the top of the Pogo, the acrid oil coat seeping into my mouth, and then I can't stop myself, I wolf it down quickly, before we even find a seat in one of the back rows of the bleachers. What difference could one little piece of deep-fried meat make?

"Guess you were hungry after all," Sol says, sitting straight up and staring ahead at the field, like an eager young boy.

"I'm always hungry," I say, trying to find what he is looking at.

"Listen, Giselle, I like hanging out in the park with you and everything and coming to Holly's meets and stuff but I was thinking, I'd like to take you out, you know, for a date, a real date. Indoors."

"I . . ."

—*No, absolutely not.*

"You what? You eat dinner, right?" He turns to me, making a loud sucking noise while sticky red, sugary ice trickles down his hand.

—*Are you actually considering going on a date?*

"Sometimes, yeah, I like Italian."

"Good, Italian it is." Sol shakes my hand formally, the deal sealed.

"OK then."

"OK then, how's Thursday?"

"Thursday's fine, no wait . . . Well, Thursday's OK, I guess."

"I'll pick you up around seven-thirty."

"Sol?" I tug at his jacket. He's turned his face into the wind, away from me.

"Yeah?"

"What's wrong?"

"Nothing. I was nervous to ask you out, I guess. I thought you'd say no. It's crazy, trying to figure you girls out." Girl. He thinks of me as a girl. For once the thought of this doesn't terrify me; that I could be someone's girl, his girl. He looks straight ahead again, blinking his long lashes. He is down to the middle of the Popsicle, where it is pure white. He wipes his hand on the bleacher and ends up with dirt on his hand.

"Why would I say no?"

He looks at me as if I am the stupidest person in the world and tries to wipe his hand on me. I laugh.

"Don't look at me like that, Solomon. And for God's sake, are you an infant? Don't wipe that on me." I push his hand away from me and deposit it on his lap.

"Sorry, something about being at a junior-high track meet brings out the idiot in me."

I take his sticky hand into mine and wrap my other arm around his shoulders. I see Saleri eyeing us from the bottom bleachers and I try to untangle myself from Sol as he approaches. I can see Saleri is nervous for Holly, like me. He smiles at me weakly and coughs into his hand.

"How's she lookin'?" I ask, gazing up at Saleri through half-closed eyes.

"Good, good. Although I'm a little worried. She was complaining about her knee yesterday. We put a tensor on it. She'll be OK I think."

"Good."

"I hear you're in med school, Gizzy. Congratulations. You always were good at science."

"Yeah, well, I just finished first year . . . I'm taking some time off . . . we'll see how it goes."

The boys' sprints and four hundred are first. Then they announce the girls' fifteen hundred. I see Holly at the side of the field stretching her legs and jumping up and down. How she hates the gun. She's the queen of false starts. Always hearing it in her head a second too soon and jumping into the air like a wild rabbit. She gives the stands a worried squint and places her white shoe on the white line.

And right before the gun goes off, she sticks her hand in her left ear to turn up the volume on her hearing aid. The gun makes a crisp snapping sound, like sticks breaking, and she falls behind Lucy, her nemesis.

Lucy's wearing a green mesh tank top with faded lettering: OLPS—Our Lady of Perpetual Sorrow. Holly stays right behind Lucy, moving with utter detachment, holding her arms stiffly, with her thumbs and fingers circled, as if she is holding acorns.

Holly is an orthodox runner and she refuses to take any risks, to expend any excess energy. One of her racing rules is to let the girl in front of her "break up all the air molecules," and so Lucy does all the work for three long laps around until Holly cuts in front of her in the last stretch. I close my eyes, feeling the greasy food settle in my contracted stomach. I hear Sol's breathing as if it were in my head.

*Oh,* he says, and, *Holly.*

I open my eyes. The white lines of the track have exploded and Holly is straddled out on the grass. Her elbows are bloody and covered with gravel, her ankle bent under her body. She gets up without looking anywhere, skilfully, automatically, as if being pulled up by some invisible cord. She leaps back onto the track. It seems I've spent my whole life watching Holly steal bases and career into asphalt.

Oh Holly.

Lucy sidesteps her cleanly, coming in first. Holly comes in second and keeps running, her hands on her hips. Saleri is at her side instantly, wiping her soaking head with a towel, pulling her arm to look at where she fell. She unravels herself from him and walks to the fence, where she finally sits down and drops her head to her knees.

Oh.

# chapter 10

Damn body never does what you want it to. Your knee stiffens and catches in the cracks, and the pain in your calf never goes away, no matter how long you stretch. The hole in your shoe lets the rain from the grass into your sock and makes your foot shrivel up so it looks like a dumb raisin afterwards. Your stupid friends at the sidelines going, "Go Holly! Go Holly!" And then there's the prayer you forget to say and remember to start when there's only thirty seconds left in the race: *Our father who art in heaven, hallowed be thy name, thy kingdom done, thy kingdom done, thy kingdom, thy kingdom.* And you're breathing out the words not breaths and God's mad at you now anyway. Then there's the start gun blasting through my head over and over like the snap of my neck cut down from a noose.

. . .

After the race I go home alone even though Sol and Giselle want to take me out for ice cream and Sol promises to buy me a Peanut Buster Parfait (my favourite) at the DQ. The house is quiet. I run a bath and sit in the tub till the water gets cold, till the skin on my toes is transparent and I can rip up the little holes in them. My feet are really awful things. Mom and Giselle keep threatening to take me for a pedicure. Once, last summer, Mom came at them with a pumice stone and a bottle of foot lotion, and after she massaged my feet, filed my toenails down, and painted them a pretty shade of pink, she held them to her face and kissed my blistered soles. Of course, not two days later I ran a cross-country race in the rain and wrecked them. Then I crawled into Mom's bed after a hot bath, showed her my chipped toenails, and asked her to redo them. "I can't always be doing these things for you, Holly, you've got to learn to do them yourself," she said. But then she sighed and asked me what colour I'd like and I picked a deep berry purple.

It seems she's right; it takes a lot of time and care to keep a body together, to be a girl. Sometimes it seems too hard, and I can't really be bothered. My hair is cropped short and when I'm not wearing my uniform I wear jeans and men's button-down shirts and sneakers. I do like baths, but the rest of it— the plucking, the shaving, the eyeliner application—it's bad enough having to watch Kat and Giselle do it. I remember being about seven and sitting on the hamper in our shared bathroom, watching Giselle do her makeup. She spent hours in front of that mirror in high school, but now she's more like me and doesn't spend a lot of time on her looks. The only concession she makes is washing her face and plucking.

"Doesn't that hurt?" I asked her as she plucked her eyebrow at a severe angle.

"It hurts like hell. Don't ever pluck or shave, Hol. If anyone can get away without doing it, it's you."

My feet are soaked enough to peel now but I feel lazy, so I turn on the hot water and splash it on my legs and wash off the cuts on my elbows and knees, then drape my legs over the edge of the tub. I make a diamond shape around my stomach with my hands, thinking about how some of Giselle's friends have their belly buttons pierced, how mine would look pretty good pierced but how Mom would probably kill me if I did something like that. Then I place my finger inside me, feeling how tight and warm I am. I feel the tender skin around the opening of my vagina; it has a name, a funny one, hymen. So much trouble and worry over such a little piece of skin that makes a woman bleed, once only. Giselle told me that in China some women put egg white on their vaginas to pretend that they're virgins. I like mine. I feel it open when I stretch my legs before I run. I wonder if you can find it after you've had sex for the first time. I'll ask Giselle. She'll probably laugh though and make some dumb joke.

"It's not afterbirth, Holly. What, you want to bury it?"

Maybe, I don't know, I'll say. There's so much fuss about sex, it seems like you should do something to mark the occasion.

The bathwater is thoroughly cold now, but I still don't want to get out so, half out of boredom, half out of curiosity, I stick my finger deep inside myself, till I can move the tip of it around. When I pull it out, a jolt of pleasure. I do it again. Hey. It's a little button, a tiny electric button. Then I spread my legs wider, my pelvis just out of the water, arched, and I rub the top again till the feeling gets more golden.

Suddenly, for some terrible reason, Sol's face is in my head, not his body or his arms but his smiling, shy face. His blue-black eyes dance at me the way they sometimes do before he makes a joke. The more I try to erase the image of his eyes watching me, the clearer it becomes, and soon I stop trying to erase it and imagine him watching me in the bathtub, how sexy I look, with my knees in the air, my hair wet and slicked back. The more swollen and wet I become, the wider his eyes get until his face is wiped away entirely, or maybe swept up in the rush of blood shooting down from my brain to the top of my legs.

Is this what love is? Having someone touch you in these tiny, hidden, wet places, without complaint? And then it's over and I can't wonder about love anymore because there's no one here but me in this terrific yellow surge of fever, throbbing through my legs, my heart.

I turn on the cold water and duck my head under the tap. Then I plug my nose and wade my head under the dirty grey water of my filth. I don't come up for air with my secret lonelies until I hear my sister banging on the door, begging to be let in.

# chapter 11

Broken bones (youths): If the bone ends are rigidly fixed together, healing occurs without callus formation. However, youths' bones take longer to achieve normal strength.

Three nights running I dream of Solomon jumping off the edge of a small cliff, wearing small paper wings just to make me laugh. Part of me is scared 'cos I think he's going to hurt himself, break every bone in his body, and part of me can't stop screaming and howling with laughter.

On the fourth night the wings begin to tear, his broad white shoulders begin to glow through the backing, his hair is dirty, he smells of tinny sweat and the sea. Then one night, instead of jumping, he walks right up to me. Kneeling beside me, he presses his hand between the folds of my skirt and, bending in, he says:

*Love me, love me more.*

# chapter 12

On Saturday I play pick-up with a bunch of older guys at the courts at school because there's a big game next week and I need to be on top of my game. Me and Chantal, a six-foot-tall black girl, are the only girls. At first the boys didn't want us to play with them but then they said it was OK.

Chantal and I are on opposite teams, so we have to cover each other. The guys have this weird way with us. For example, if we travel or double-dribble they won't call us on it, or, if we get knocked down by a good block they'll yell, "Foul!" and one of us gets to take a shot. But this favouritism also has a downside because they're always telling us what to do, like we don't know the rules of basketball or something.

Roy, who just missed a perfect layup, tries to blame it on me by saying, "You should've been roving the key, Holly. You weren't there."

Roving the key my ass. *You* rove the key! Chantal and I usually suck it up. We just roll our eyes at each other, but Chantal had had enough: "Screw you, Roy! Me 'n Hol are always *roving,* pass us the ball for a change. Make it worth our while."

Today is our big tournament downtown. I can't decide if I love or hate these inner-city games. Riding on a yellow school bus all morning just to get your ass kicked by girls who can outrun, outshoot, outreach you, every time, is kind of depressing. They're good. They're fast. And if you try to foul or slap the ball away you're finished.

Jen gets fouled out by the second period and I can tell by all the teeth-sucking and cussing going on, on both sides, that there is going to be trouble after the game. I think even Saleri, who is usually clueless, can sense it too.

"Go on home, Jen," he says.

"Fuck 'em." Jen sits down beside me, massaging her fingers, thinking she's so butch, so tough.

Saleri lets me play in the last two periods even though my knee is acting screwy and nothing goes right. The other team keeps slapping the ball out of my hands and we keep missing passes and blaming each other. It's a mess, really hopeless. We lose by twenty points. I can feel the hair on the back of my neck stand up in straight, sweaty spikes.

And sure enough, after the game, the other team sends a messenger into our locker room.

"They're waiting for you in the parking lot!" a small grade-six girl with thick glasses yells before hightailing it out of our change room. I meet Jen's eyes. Her eyebrows go up.

"Did someone say rumble? Yeah! They're on!" Jen yells, slamming her locker shut and slapping my back. Full of anger about losing the game, Jen's got an excess of energy suddenly. "What do you say, Hol? You in?"

"I don't know, Jen, they're, like, pretty huge girls."

"We can take 'em."

We limp outside like a bunch of soldiers, Jen in front jumping around, ready for a scrap. Kat lags back a bit, looking scared, watching the other girls swarm around us.

"Hey, losers." A tall girl with long black hair and beady eyes appears in front of me and pushes my chest. I push back, my heart suddenly in my throat.

"Don't touch my fucking girl," Jen says, exploding from behind me like an unleashed dog. Something inside me is trembling, shaking, until the guard on the other team steps forward and snatches Jen up by the collar of her coat, like in an old gangster movie.

I am tired in my eyes. The world is without colour except for the white maddening motion of the guard's jacket up against Jen. Her knuckle under Jen's chin looks like a rock and I hook my arm through Jen's thinking if I can keep her next to me it will be OK. OK . . .

But there's another girl on top of me by then and the others are receding like they're running backwards, slowly, their running shoes kicking my face, the smell of rubber and scum in my skull and then, out of nowhere, there's, like, five girls jumping on us at the same time. Me and Jen, still tangled, collapse onto the pavement, crushed at the bottom of the pile. But then I am cut from her, am alone, in the air, landing on cold metal.

Then Saleri's voice and the smell of blood in my broken nose. In my eyes a warm liquid pain, feeling the tread of someone's shoe on my chest. Someone grabbing my hair, yelling at me but I can't hear them. I can't hear anything except Mr. Saleri's calm voice and the whoosh of blood in my ears.

I'm on top of a car. Can't move. Jen's face hovering and Saleri pulling me up by the arms and leading me to another car, asking, "What happened? What happened? What happened! Who started this? You girls, you girls . . ."

And all I can do is fold my hand over my face to keep it from leaking out, to keep it arranged and contained in my hand and Saleri saying: "Jesus, Jesus, JesusChrist." He's starting up the car and I know Kat and Jen are in the back seat, all quiet-like, and this, along with Mr. Saleri's taking the Lord's name in vain, gets me worried, so I try pulling the mirror down to see if I look like a fucking Picasso painting or what and there's a leak that feels like a sparkler just exploded in my nose and blood, ah blood, so I don't even get to see how messed up my face is 'cos my chest feels like it's collapsing.

Though my nose is broken, I don't cry on the way to the hospital. I don't cry either when the doctor sticks his fingers in the cracked and searing regions of my chest, saying, "This won't hurt a bit." And then there's a roll of thunder in my head and the world is a tunnel. And then I am finally home free.

. . .

The hardest thing about being in the hospital is having to sleep over, alone. After Dad died, Giselle and I started sleeping with Mom almost every night. Most nights Giselle slept turned away from me but sometimes she and I would face each other, curled up on one side of the bed, our fingers locked together.

When Dad was alive, sometimes all four of us would sleep in their bed: me tucked safely under his arm and Giselle curled around Mom's hip. If we were camping or on holiday, we'd push all the mattresses together. My father would tell us stories until we dropped away to sleep, or he would tell weird jokes Giselle and I never got.

When we were kids and we'd come climbing onto them like little animals, clawing our way into their soft flannel warmth, Mom would laugh loudly at my father's standard joke: here he was, thousands of miles away from his peasant upbringing, and still sleeping with his children. We'd all, especially my mother, laugh hysterically, as if it were the first time we had heard it.

"Dammit, girls, why'd I spend so much money on beds?" he'd say, pretending to be annoyed, shifting his body and pulling my knees onto the mattress so my too-long legs wouldn't hang off the bed.

"You know, it's too bad we don't have a goat, because the goat could sleep with us too. And look at this one," he'd say, picking me up by the ankles while I squealed with delight. "Wearing socks to bed! And mismatched! One red, one green! A regular gypsy princess!"

We slept like animals, rolling into their arms with our grizzly girl dreams. Giselle and I were just happy that they never kicked us out of their room when we crept in late at night, worried about something, sick, or not tired enough to sleep.

I liked the mornings best, when Giselle and I would pretend to sleep and they covered us with their duvets. He'd sit there stroking my calf, or my hair, drinking his coffee, the smell of his strong black espresso filling the room, waiting for Mom to return from the shower and, when she did, she'd move to the other side of the room to dry herself. With my eyes half-open, I'd watch her put on her clothes. I was fascinated by the dark Caesarean scar weaving its way from her pubic hair to her belly button, marking my entry into the world. Then I'd slant my half-closed eyes across the room and pretend I was asleep, that I didn't hear their soft voices murmuring about the day ahead, about us, in a language I couldn't understand.

After he died, we didn't laugh at all about goats or socks and gypsies. Most nights, I'd just hold Mom's hand, while she lay there staring at the ceiling and Giselle turned her back to us. And our mourning, which had been a sharp and stinging absence at first, became a dull ache.

When I started junior high, and joined the basketball team, I also started falling asleep on the couch with the TV on.

"I left your breakfast on the table and some money for juice on the counter," Mom would say, touching my shoulder. "It's almost eight-thirty." And I'd slip from sleep into my mother's brown eyes each morning, a pain in my neck from sleeping in a sitting position.

"Mama, why are we so sad?" I'd whisper as she pulled her hand through my hair.

The first night Giselle came back from the hospital, she eyed me strangely when I sat in Mom's bed reading a comic book. "Don't you think it's time you slept on your own, Hol?"

I shook my head and tried to ignore her. But that night, Giselle, wrapped in a sheet, crawled in between Mom and I. "I'm so cold," she whispered, though it was May and already warm.

And as I stroked my sister's bony shivering spine, I felt the down, the soft white anorexic hair that had grown there to protect her when she'd slept alone all those nights away.

Now, like her, I am in this hospital room alone. If I close my eyes long enough and do not move at all, it is like I am nothing. It is not sleep, and not a quiet prayer. It is just disappearing, with no sound or heat or pain. Out of time, an absence. I am absent. In this room.

# chapter 13

Strapping broken ribs is discouraged.

After the call, Mom and I go to the hospital in silence. We walk through the brightly lit halls, down to the children's section, where Holly is sitting up, stoned on painkillers. There's a bandage over her nose and she's arranged on a pile of pillows. I check to make sure they haven't strapped her ribs. She has a wan smile on her face and says, "Hey!" a little too cheerily as we pull chairs up next to her bed.

Mom's face is riddled ... with what? I can't tell anymore. Perhaps a mixture of anger and relief, or simply the exhaustion of someone used to hearing bad news. But she's smiling too as she takes Holly's hand and mine in the other.

I am the first to speak, reaching out to stroke Holly's hair. "You OK?"

"Yeah." She tries to smile but her chapped lips crack.

"Don't ask me what happened. Whatever. Don't."

Holly looks straight ahead at the drawing of Winnie-the-Pooh scooping honey from a jar. It's not a very good depiction: old Winnie looks like a jaundiced, jovial rat.

But I wasn't planning on asking. I know the aggression of Catholic girls in Holly's world, how they love to fight. It was my world too, for all of grade school and high school; seven long years of untenable hell. I also know what Holly is capable of: I've seen her do handstands on gravel, belly flop off a six-foot diving board. Holly lives for this stuff, but then I'm surprised because she starts talking, slowly, in her old-Holly baby voice:

"I'm sorry, Mommy. So sorry."

Injuries known as "crash injuries" are due to severe pressure.

While Holly stays in the hospital overnight, Sol takes me to a nice Italian place in the east end. He looks handsome; he's clean-shaven and smells of soap, though he manages to spill red wine on his shirt before we've even ordered food. He's even gotten his cast off and shows off his dextrous wrist by rotating it in circles over the table. It looks thinner and paler than his other wrist.

"Did it hurt when they cut it off?"

"Naw, but I hate hospitals. Makes me nervous being in one, no offence."

"I know. Most people don't like hospitals. I keep thinking of Holly, looking so small in that blue hospital gown. I keep thinking of her nose," I say as Sol peruses the menu. I don't look. I already know what I want. I always order the same thing at good Italian places: mussels in white wine sauce and garlic bread. Filling, but the lowest possible calorie count.

"Did you find out at least if Holly got some punches in?"

I shake my head. "No, she likes to do daredevil stuff. This one time she tried to jump off the roof into the driveway through the basketball net. But she doesn't like to fight people. Except me, of course."

"So, when's she coming back?"

"Tomorrow, or maybe the day after. They say she landed on her head, well, her face, really, so they want to keep her for observation."

He nods.

My glass misses my mouth and I end up spilling water on my face. Sol takes his napkin and wipes it off.

"I miss your hair," he says. I've got it wrapped up in a blue scarf tonight, presentable.

"Oh, I used to have really great hair, not to be vain, but I take pride in five things in life—my studying skills, my hair, and . . ."

The waiter arrives with a dish of spiced olives, garlic bread, and a steaming plate of Alfredo pasta. He uncorks another bottle of wine, pours a glass, and offers it to me. I take a sip.

—*We used to have beautiful hair. We.*

So it begins. I panic about the food: three olives, almost a hundred calories, if you round up. Sol starts to pile the pasta on my plate and a sweat breaks out on my forehead.

"I didn't order this! I can't eat it."

"I ordered it . . . relax," Sol says, giving me a sharp look.

—*He's upsetting, upsetting the balance of everything. Everything's been calculated, planned out, and then he comes in and—*

I pop two more olives into my mouth and try not to think too much about it, what the hell, it's a special occasion. It's a date, for God's sake, and, in some ways, my first proper one. But at the back of my spine I feel a humming, and as he continues to load pasta on my plate I practically yell, "That's enough!"

Sol looks around at the people at the tables next to us who smile nervously back at him, twirling their pasta on their forks. The waiter asks us if everything is all right and Sol nods and refills our glasses with wine. After the waiter leaves, Sol leans towards me. "You wanna tell me why you're so on edge?"

"Not really, I want to eat, let's just eat, OK?" I say, my mouth half-full of pasta and two salty olive pits lodged under my tongue.

"Don't you like this place?" he asks, picking up his fork and letting his dark eyes fall on my naked shoulders. "I thought you were *always* hungry."

"I am. Love pasta," I say, shovelling a forkful into my mouth, wondering how many I can manage before pushing the plate away and excusing myself to the washroom.

Etiology: 1) the study of origin, specifically termed in medicine as the science of disease; 2) used, in a more general, non-medical sense, to term assigning of cause.

Holly's coming back today, so Mom and I are trying to do some kind of spring cleaning, though it's already the beginning of June. She's mopping the floors and I'm standing on a chair trying to unhook the curtains from the rod so we can wash them.

When Mom and I are alone in the house, with hours spread before us without having to go shopping, or pick Holly up from some practice, or drive me to some appointment, I like to ask her about her past, about Thomas, and about her boyfriend, her fiancé, I should say, before Dad. I know some pieces of the story. I know that the fiancé's name was Misha. That she was supposed to marry Misha, but he died four months before the date. The part about Dad—how they met and fell in love—is vague. Will learning about the past help me understand what happened to Thomas and me? Why we failed?

Perhaps the scientist in me is desperate to locate the source of our unhappiness with each other. Maybe I need a fairy tale about my parents' courtship to believe in. For whatever reason, I'm curious, I'm compelled to ask questions, to gather evidence about my unfinished business with my father before my case is complete. This never-ending dossier I add to, subtract from, invent invisible paperwork for, this dossier labelled Love—I carry it with me everywhere.

Although I've heard the story too many times to count, I need to hear it again. Each time I feel that I miss something. Mom's storytelling is like watching an old movie. Maybe it's her accent, or the fact that she's translating and I have to pay more attention to the colloquial, because, in all the ephemera—the wit and flirting and costume changes—I've somehow lost track of what's really going on. It's a game Mom and I play: she warms up to it slowly, she pretends she is revealing cabal information and I prompt her, faking ignorance though I can anticipate every part of the story. She looks up from the floor and leans the mop against the counter when I speak.

"So, tell me again about the sanatorium, but tell me about before too, when you were a nurse in Hungary."

She shrugs, then goes to the sink and pours herself a small tumbler of clear apricot liquor, takes a sip and pours me one, too. We clink glasses and then she tilts her head.

I cringe as the sweet alcohol, the taste of my mother's courage, burns down my throat.

"What do you want to know?"

"Why. Why you went to the sanatorium."

She holds the bottle up to the light, checking to see, maybe, if there is enough liquid to finish her story.

"I met your father at one of Misha's parties, in Hungary. He was drunk, your father, not Misha, and was slurring his words. He was tall and had the most amazing blue eyes, and wore poor clothes and all the women laughed when he told his crazy stories. Anyway, it was a dinner party and, after dessert, I was in the dining room, arranging the flowers I'd ordered for the party.

"He came up behind me. I could see him coming because there was a mirror and I should have turned away but I didn't. I stayed there, smelling the lilies, waiting to see what he would do. He stood behind me for a good couple of minutes. No one even noticed us, standing there, looking at our reflection. He was standing there, inhaling me like I was the flowers. And I could smell the liquor on him, I could smell the sweat on his clothes and the cigars Misha fosted on him."

"It's *foisted*, Mom, foisted . . . Anyway, did he say something? What did he want?" It never fails, I'm always outraged and thrilled by Thomas's indiscretion. I open the fridge and get us two beers, pour them into glasses and squeeze lemon in, the way Mom likes it. We move out onto the front porch where the sun is shining. The floor is drying and the curtains are in the wash on delicate, so we have time. She sits in the swinging chair at the edge of the porch and I sit next to her. She puts her arm around me.

"Cheers," I say, smiling. Mom smiles back, licking the beer sweat off the edge of her glass.

"So, what happened?"

"Your father said, 'What are you doing here? You don't belong here, and you can't convince anyone, not even him.' So I turned around and slapped him."

"What did he mean you didn't belong there? You were going to *marry* Misha."

Mom slides her eyes over to me as if I've caught her on something but she gathers herself quickly.

"I guess he meant, politically, socially."

"So what does that mean? That you weren't a Communist? That he was out of your league?"

"Something like that. Let's just say I wasn't the ideal wife for Misha."

"But—"

"You can't understand it, I know. I was a nurse, Giselle, just a nurse."

I laugh. "What do you mean, 'just a nurse'? Isn't that the point of socialism, that everyone's equal?"

"Yes, Giselle, in theory, in a perfect world, as they say, but not in practice."

"I don't understand."

"Look, it wasn't just that, as a student I was involved in a couple of anti-regime protests, clubs . . ."

"And you gave all that up when you met Misha?"

Mom gives me a cutting look and leans towards me, speaking slowly.

"I can't explain it to you. I can't justify it. Things were not like they are now. I met a man, a good one, despite his politics, then I met your father. So, do you want to hear the end of the story or not?"

Suddenly I understand that the more questions I ask Mom, the less she'll talk. That although I've grown up to the hum of her voice explaining the old world to me, the context of the forces that guided her will always remain mysterious.

"You, Giselle, are my daughter. You can listen to my stories, but you cannot judge."

I nod. "OK."

"Misha came running over," she continues. "He tried to smooth over the situation. He said he thought Thomas had had too much to drink. Misha hugged me, in front of everyone. I'd caused a minor scandal in the presence of his colleagues, but he was kind." She turns to me and studies my eyes, as if she sees something in my face she wants to describe, needs to talk about.

"Your father wasn't a bad man, Giselle."

I take the glass hanging loosely from my mother's hand and meet her gaze.

"I know, Ma, so what happened?"

"They kicked your father out on the street, like in cartoons, on his ass."

"God!"

"Yes. But there was a letter in the flowers with an address on it. He was going to work in a sanatorium, he'd come there to tell Misha that he was going away."

"But then he got distracted? By you?"

My mother flushes and talks into her hands.

"There's something I've not told you before. I knew Thomas before I met Misha. We went to high school together, only he was just graduating when I began school. He knew I had started nursing school, he knew my father, my mother . . ."

"Whoa. What do you mean you *knew him*? You knew Dad before you even met Misha?"

She ignores my question and rests her head on the top of my head as we sway into the last part of the afternoon. "Your father never got invited back. Thomas was Misha's personal doctor, but Misha died not long after that big scene, their goodbye, I guess. That's why I followed your father to the sanatorium, to get away from everyone, and everything," she says, as if it's all clear, as if it's all completely logical.

My mother picks up her head and sniffs the air, turning away so that I can't see her eyes: story's over. She rocks the chair with her heels. I think about how she says his name over and over, pushing out the edges of her lips and shifting her eyes away. *Misha*. Quickly, so fast, I could almost pretend I didn't hear the rapture catching in her throat like a sob.

Generation time for TB is relatively normal for a highly contagious disease under unsanitary conditions. Transmission is via airborne droplet infection: coughing, sneezing, and singing can transmit it.

Sol arrives in a beat-up old Chevy just as Mom is pulling out to go pick Holly up from the hospital. Sol goes over to the car and introduces himself through the window. Mom gives him a big smile and then I can see her winking at me and giving me the thumbs-up all the way down the street. I have a feeling I know what she will say later: "Gizella, you did not tell me he was so warm. He's warm!"

"You mean hot, Mom . . . Yes, he's handsome."

I take my feet out of Holly's sneakers and snake them through the grass as Sol flops down next to me and kisses my cheek.

"That was relatively painless."

"I think my mother thinks you're good-looking."

"Well, can't say I blame her." Sol plucks the beer bottle out of my hand and takes a swig, then he tries to smell my armpit.

"Hey!"

"You smell good, like bleach and grass and sweat. Like tennis shoes and beer and lemon." He steals another kiss—a long one. My head gets dizzy when he does that. I haven't eaten anything all day except an old lead-heavy zucchini muffin Holly brought home from her home ec class, leaving the French toast Mom made me in the oven to dry out.

"What's on your mind, G.? You seem distracted."

I look at Sol's eyes, sombre and full of longing. I notice how when the light hits them they aren't black at all, but almost hazel, warm, trusting. Suddenly, I'm filled with dread. The thought of going on with the rest of the afternoon, let alone the rest of my life, is overwhelming.

"I don't know, I think I need another drink. I think you need one, too."

Sol jumps up. "I'll get them, just one though. There's a police press conference I gotta go to soon."

When he comes back with two beers, we clink bottles and I grab his hand and he kisses me again, filling up my delicate confusion with his sunshine mouth until the dog next door starts barking ferociously.

"Sol?"

"Yeah?"

"I think my mother had an affair," I say, staring straight ahead at the dead-end cracked grey concrete of our quiet little street, willing the dog to stop.

"What? With who?" Sol gets down on one knee and bends his head, listening, ever listening.

"With our dad."

# chapter 14

I'm standing at the window of the hospital room, waiting for our car to come into the parking lot. It's a beautiful day. I picture Jen and everybody kicking a soccer ball around and wonder if Marco has even noticed that I'm gone. The pain's not so bad today and I'm feeling less groggy. I put on my uniform—the only clothes that I can see are around—there's still blood on my collar and shirt front. I can't find my socks so I put on a pair of paper hospital socks and then my shoes. When I finally see Mom, a nurse comes in with a wheelchair and my file.

"Do I really have to?"

She nods and smiles and then places my knapsack, full of books and sneakers and damp clothes, in my lap. She wheels me out to the entrance, where Mom's waiting, looking a little red. Her hair's all messed up and when she kisses me she smells grainy, like Dad used to smell after coming home late at night after staff parties.

"Are you all right?" I ask her. "You seem weird."

"I'm not, I'm fine."

I walk to the car, slowly 'cos it hurts to move too fast, to breathe too deep. Mom holds my arm and looks down at the ground.

She starts the engine and takes the first turn a little wide.

"Am I in trouble?"

Mom slants her eyes at me.

"For what?"

"For this, the hospital, the fight."

Mom looks at the road as she speeds up to stop at a red.

"No, Holly, you're not in trouble."

"Because you can ask Mr. Saleri, you can ask Jen, Ma . . . Look, those girls just jumped on us."

Mom nods and glances down at her hands, which are red and raw.

"I know, honey, I'm believing you."

"You do?"

"Yeah."

We stop at a dessert shop and Mom has coffee and a glazed nut cake and I order cheesecake and a Coke. Mom stares at me as I gulp it down.

"Do you feel all right? Do you have any pain?"

I nod and continue eating the cake.

"Yours is better, your cheesecake. This thing tastes like a box."

Mom looks so worried and messy, like she needs to be comforted, so I reach out my hand and she takes it, open-palmed.

"I need you to promise me one thing though, Holly."

I throw my fork down. "I told you! It was messed up, *we* were the losers, they'd already beaten us, why would we—"

"It's not about that. I need you to finish high school. I know you don't like it, but you have to try."

I pick up my fork. "They have a hockey team in high school."

Mom laughs, "No hockey. Pick two sports, just two."

"Can't I pick hockey?"

But Mom doesn't hear my question. She's staring into the grains of her espresso cup, and then, without looking at me, she says, "We're a family. Aren't we?"

I don't say anything, mushing the crumbs of my cake onto my fork. Then a group of university students comes in. The girls are Giselle's age. They're wearing cool black and beige clothes and their crisp, citrusy smell fills the warm shop instantly. They all have long, silky blond hair, and their faces are round and pink. Everything about them seems soft to touch. They open their schoolbooks while the boys with them go to the counter. I can't stop staring at the girls. They all seem to have big eyes that roll around a lot as they talk to each other. They seem so constructed, so put-together; their looks and clothes are so alien compared to Giselle's angles, the holes in her socks and jeans. I think about Giselle's big, raw-boned gestures, how mannish she is.

I think about how, sometimes at night, I remember a stupid joke I heard at school that I forgot to tell Mom and Giselle, and then I start thinking about all the trips we still need to take, all the living left for us in the same house, how time might be running out. I want to tell Mom about those floating night thoughts and jokes and plans and worries but somehow I can't assemble it. And I can't tell her about his ghost. Although he has no fear of endings, and watches us from a dark corner of the sky.

# chapter 15

Students of medicine will learn to respect boundaries (i.e., learn the appreciation of differences between personal and professional roles) in the doctor-patient relationship.

I wake up to Holly kicking my bare feet with her tennis shoe. Sol is nowhere to be seen. She pushes her kilt down between her knees as she sits and I remember then that we forgot to bring Holly any other clothes while she was in the hospital.

"What you guys been doing?" She pulls a dried piece of grass and puts it in her mouth.

"Sleeping."

She nods and squints into the fading sun. "Mama been telling you her stories?"

I nod, then reach over to grip the long blades of grass to get myself up.

"We gotta mow this crazy lawn."

Holly nods, spitting pieces of grass out of her mouth. "Don't worry, your new boyfriend already said he'd do it. Geez, how much did you guys drink?"

"Not much," I say, kicking the bottles as I raise myself up on my arms.

"I gotta go," Sol says, coming out of the house, smiling. "But I'll be back later to check up on our patient." He winks at Holly. "How are you doing?"

"Still hurts, no long jump for a while, that's for sure."

We go in and Mom's making dinner, Holly's favourite: potato salad and tofu dogs with macaroni and cheese. I eat a couple of bites, but feel too upset to eat much, so I finish the floor, iron the curtains, and Mom falls asleep on the couch, in front of the eleven o'clock news.

Later that night, Holly comes into my room, where I am staring at old X-rays from school and still trying to process the fact that Mom knew Thomas before Misha. I don't know where to put this information, where and how to file it in my case against him. The implications are tremendous.

Holly stands in my doorway, freshly showered. Her hair has grown out from her severe crewcut and she's got it slicked back. She's in her favourite outfit: a sports bra and Dad's pyjama bottoms. Her foot's hooked against her ankle, her chest is bruised, purple-blue butterflies bloom beneath the white cotton of her bra, the lowest part of the wing reaching out to her taut belly button. She stands there sniffing her armpits. Holly's bigger than me, wider hips and shoulders. She also probably weighs about ten or fifteen pounds more than me, all lean muscle. She's nicely proportioned, her breasts look full and perky at the same time, everything about Holly is strong. Seeing her, I wonder how it is that I can look at her and see skinny but when I look at myself I see a bloated mess.

"C'mere, stinky."

"What? I just had a shower."

I touch the bruises lightly. "You want something for it?"

"No, I'm OK . . . it's kinda cool hey? Like those psychology ink pictures."

"Yeah."

Holly looks down the hall. "Should I bother waking her up for bed?"

"No."

She juts her chin out, defiantly, words pushing at the bottom of her lip.

"What is it, Hol?"

"When I go back next week, I gotta write this math test, a final. I suck at math. I suck so hard, Giselle."

"What about your teacher?"

"Yeah, she explains it all and does the questions but then, when I'm alone, doing a test or something . . . I just forget it. I just don't have that math-brain gene. It's missing in me, I think. I'm gonna ask to bring it home, you know."

I laugh, "And I'm going to write your grade-eight math exam?"

"But the numbers, they get all screwy, and now I missed all this school, so I have no idea what's going on . . ."

She stretches her long body up and grips the top of the doorway; I count her ribs.

"So, you'll do it?"

"I'll show you how. Tonight, come on, bring your books in."

Holly blows out a frustrated breath. "What about Sol?"

"Sol's terrible at math, come on, Holly."

"Come on what? I'm not going to be a doctor or an accountant, it doesn't matter." She's clenching her jaw now, grinding her teeth together.

"But there are basic things you need to know that you don't. You won't be able to get through high school even, when the time comes."

"Were you good at math?"

"Not really."

"So?"

"So, what?"

"Get up," she says, pulling on my arm.

"Stop it," I say, trying to wrench myself away.

"Get up and look at me."

I stand up, trying to extend my spine so I can match Holly's height.

"Look at me."

"I'm looking."

"Look at me, at this."

Holly plunges her hand into her hair and pulls out her hearing aid. She slaps it on my desk. Then she sweeps her arm along my desk, pushing everything onto the floor. I get scared that she's going to try to throw me across the room again, or hurt me, so I start backing away, but instead she just stands there and cries:

"I can't do school, Giselle, I can't do it. I can barely hear the teachers. I can read and write on my own but I can't do it, do you understand me? Do you know what that's like?" she yells, a little too loud now, without her ear.

The piece has become part of her, literally wedged into the side of her head. It's small, shell-shaped, beige-brown, dirty with age and wear. It's creepy, it looks like what it is: a spliced organ missing from the body and made external, the transparent wires dispatching sound-words.

Holly's slit-eyes stare at me and, with her mouth slightly open, she looks like she did when she was very young. Suddenly, I am transported:

It's late at night and no matter how many pillows I pile over my head I can hear our father's sobbing through the thin walls of our suburban house. There's nothing worse than hearing a grown man cry, I think inside my twelve-year-old head. This is the day they have finally taken Holly to the specialist who has diagnosed her with a hearing problem and a slight learning disability. And no matter how many times our mother says, *It doesn't matter, Thomas, can't you see, she is perfect?* he won't listen and keeps crying.

When Holly can't sleep with Mom and Dad, like tonight, she sleeps with me, sprawled all over my single bed, her long hair spilling into my mouth, but she can't hear his sobbing.

*Shut up. Oh please please please please please please stopit.*

And no matter how many Magic-Markered pictures of our happy family she brings home from junior kindergarten, no matter how many King-of-the-Family gold-sprayed macaroni crowns she makes him with Ts on them, no matter how many endless hours I spend teaching Holly how to hold her mouth to form vowels, filling her with the names of animals, colours, and numbers, disappointment continues to collect in the wrinkles in his brows and ages his long, handsome face.

One day, after months of constant badgering and trickery on my part and so much candy that half of Holly's baby teeth have gone rotten, it has all, finally, paid off. A miracle: Holly learns to read six months into senior kindergarten—almost a full year before the rest of her mud-poking peers and, in the meantime, I have been bumped up a grade; I have become such a precocious child that the teachers are loath to have me in their classes.

"Look, Papa, the doctor was wrong."

We are in the living room, my hands on Holly's shoulders. I push her forward to read him a short paragraph from a children's book about how even spiders have bad days and, when she's finished, he opens his arms and she crawls into them. He nuzzles the plastic beneath her hair, then folds his body over hers. I shift from foot to foot on the dirty hardwood floor, feeling awkward.

He looks up. His eyes examine my oily preteen moon face. He looks at my little nipples poking through my washed-out

Mickey Mouse T-shirt, my strong arms. He fixes his eyes on my thick calves: the result of riding up hills on a broken bicycle in high gear, the cost of being big-boned. My squat little in-between body is still waiting for the legendary Vasco genes that should kick in any day now and stretch out this tightly packed mass of muscle and fat and make me long and lean like the rest of them. I smile at him proudly, waiting for compliments on my patience and dedication to rain down on me. Waiting.

Then he does something awful. He reaches out and squeezes my thick leg, pinching the fat next to the knee. It is meant to be a playful gesture, maybe, I don't know. And then I do an awful thing too. I lean over and say right in his face:

"You piece of *shit*." I turn on my heel and run out the front door before he can catch up to beat me within an inch of my life as if we are in the old country where children can be poked and pinched and thrashed like barn animals.

He dies three weeks later and Mom takes leave from work so she can sit at home like a zombie. Holly is put in the advanced reading group at school, and takes speech classes twice a week and writes haikus about frogs and heaven.

And I grow three and a half inches the month after Thomas dies.

Bodily wounds may be classified according to the mode of damage.

Holly reinserts her hearing aid and then lies down on my bed silently, touching the soft flannel on the edge of my sheet while I pile the books back on my desk.

"Sorry for throwing your stuff." Holly's eyes glaze over. She seems very tired suddenly.

"Listen, we'll do something, I'll ask Mom to get you a tutor, we'll get your ears retested. But Holly, and don't get mad at me for saying this, you can't blame this on your hearing."

"Why not?"

I make a face. "Because, lazy-ass, you're acing English, because, somehow, miraculously, your batteries only seem to die during math class."

Holly throws a pillow at me.

"Am I right?"

"No!" She peeks out at me through the sheet.

"I don't believe you."

"Look, I don't really care. I just don't want everyone freaking out when I flunk junior-high math, is all."

"Nobody's flunking anything. Do you want to go to summer school?" Holly makes a barfing sound.

"OK, so turn on your hearing aid."

I pause, about to ask her about something else, when she leans herself out of bed, splays one hand on the floor and asks, "Did she tell you? About how she got him kicked out of the house?"

My back arches, I crawl over to her, pull her half on the bed, half off the bed, body to me. I hold her up to my face but her eyes slip away from mine again.

"You know that story, Mom's told you before?"

Holly shakes her head, her lids slide closed. "I've never heard it from Mom, I heard it from Dad."

"Dad?"

"Yup. Daddy tells me everything," she says, her eyes half-closed.

"That's right, I forgot, you talk to ghosts."

"Just his."

"So, who do you think she loved more?"

"Dad," Holly says, without missing a beat.

"Dad? Why Dad?"

"Why *not* Dad?"

Holly lies back down on the bed and turns away, tracing her fingers over the flower patterns in the wallpaper. Before she passes out, I get her to take out her hearing aid again to do an informal ear examination. She cups her hand over the right side of her head and I drop my books on the floor.

"Can you hear that?"

"Well, sort of."

"What do you mean, *sort of*?"

"I can hear it in my feet."

"In your feet?"

"Well, yeah, the vibrations."

"OK, go to bed, baby."

When she's bundled in my sheets and has her head against the wall, I look at the tiny piece of plastic, the source of so many of Holly's and Dad's frustrations. The reason she moves through the world intuitively: touching, feeling, falling into the space around her, careening brightly from sky to earth to floor. I pick up the greasy bit of plastic and try to read her, to feel out her aches, her longings, from that battered little machine that helps her think.

And I think about Thomas, again, how Holly could be persuaded to do anything, possibly even pass grade-eight math, if he were still around.

When we were young he used to take us fishing. He woke us early in the morning, offering cups of hot chocolate as consolation for waking us up. We'd drive about an hour out of the city, then he'd park by a lakefront, take the canoe off the top of the car, and paddle us to the darkest part of the shore. He'd burn through the ends of the plastic lines with the butt of his cigarette and tie our hooks on carefully. Around this time I'd wake up and start chatting, asking him questions.

"How come those sunfish have pointy things on top that hurt so much?"

"I dunno, Giselle, but you're being quiet or you'll scare the fish."

I could never stay quiet for long. I'd start imitating the morning bird calls and pestering him.

"Why can't we keep that one?"

"Too small . . . a good fisherman knows what to keep, what to throw back."

A good fisherman I was not. After a couple of Saturday mornings of rocking the canoe and exhausting both of them with my questions and squawking, I gave up, and only Holly went with him.

Look at this picture: a voiceless three-year-old patiently watching her father cast his line into the warm velvet morning water. She is wearing a white Gilligan hat, her nose is freckled from the sun. She is staring intently at the red-and-white buoy on the surface. Her father is wearing a white undershirt, his face sweaty, his doctor-hands are soiled with worm-dirt and grease and the eternal cigarette dangles from his mouth. He accidentally blows smoke into her face.

But Holly never complains. She cannot hear the birds, or his swearing when he tugs too quickly and yanks the hook out of a bass's mouth and tangles his line. Doesn't want to sing, like in the daycare when they make her and her voice comes out screeching and high. She doesn't question anything he does because it makes sense: the shore, the trees, the muck at the bottom of the canoe, his cigarette smoke, his fishy, musky smell. It is all she understands.

He brings in the line and when she sighs in quiet frustration he paddles away from shore; the wind has blown them too close now.

Hours later, when they are brown and tired and happy with the modest, white-bellied bass, fat enough for four but not too many to anger the god of good fishermen, later, they come home. Me and Mom stand on the porch in our aprons, our faces dusty with the pies we have baked.

After dinner, Holly sits on his lap while he bounces her on his knee, knocking her around as if she were riding a jittery pony. She tries to open her drooping eyes, because the family is happy and laughing and full—the salty lemon taste of fish melting in our mouths, we are saying her name: *Holly Bolly Polly Holly. Girl! Wake up! There's strawberry pie! Your favourite!*

Sucking on a rubbery fish skeleton, seeing us from his eyes, she kicks out her leg, flings her arms wide, about to hug the world.

Holly throws herself into the air. Flying. Climbing over Dad, thrashing her limbs at him: she jumps.

Never hesitating for a moment that she will be caught.

And staring at that stupid, too-small hearing aid, I start to cry. For Holly, who lost the man who loved her best, for Mom, who lost them both, for our warped little suburban trinity of women that won't hear a man's step on the stairway, or his cough in the night, or ever taste the paprika stew he made in the winter when none of us was home and he listened to gypsy music at top volume. I cry for myself, because I don't even know which man to start mourning. Loss doubled, loss tripled, loss endlessly multiplying is infinite.

*You had the chance to love me, but you gave it up. Is it true? Or was it your only way?* I stare at the monkey skull Thomas gave me after I had perused his travelling kit one too many times. I once used his scissors and knives to bury little birds and squirrels in our backyard. I received a terse slap from Thomas and a lecture on sterilization and the potential dangers I could be inflicting on his patients. I stood in front of him sniffling, apologizing.

Feeling sorry for me, Thomas leaned over, still wearing his green scrubs, smelling like the hospital, sterile but like a toilet. He held out the one object I could have: a tiny monkey skull.

"Use this for your little explorations. Don't touch my stuff," he said before pushing me out of the room.

I remember the first time I held the little skull, feeling its weight in my hands. Besides the Christmas and birthday presents bought by Mom from both of them, it was the only gift Thomas had ever given me. Holly, dressed in a pink velour jumpsuit, sensed my fascination with the object, and intent on possession, grabbed it from me with her sticky hands. But I'd had the skull clutched next to my heart, and she couldn't get at it. In a loud clear voice I said:

"This is *mine*."

Holly pulled her hands behind her back obediently and, nodding at me in a businesslike way, moved on through the living room.

*This is mine. This is*—my brain repeats, making words from the sobs that wrench up like chunks of diamonds caught in my esophagus . . . *this, this is you*. And the last time I let him get to me.

—*This is it, we are even. And you are dead.*

# chapter 16

They think, the kids at school, they think I'm nuts. Today, my first day back, I climbed the ten-foot wire fence that wraps around the schoolyard. I don't know why I did it but it scared me, that stupid fence, with the barbed wire at the top poking up into the sky. So, at lunchtime, I just went up it.

"What're you doing?" Jen said, putting her hands on her hips. "Get the hell off, someone's going to see you." But there was ringing in my ears and the gauze on my ribs was itching me 'cos Giselle didn't wake up early enough to get me in the shower and by then some other kids were standing around watching so I had to do it.

When I got to the top, I gripped the barbs, bent my knees back, and turned around to face the crowd. Mr. Saleri was standing in front, looking up at me.

"Holly, I want you to come on down now."

"OK, sir, just wanted to see if I could do it."

I tried to wave at him but the barbs poked into my hands and shot spikes of heat up my spine. I lowered myself, facing them, gripping each square piece of the fence tightly. About five feet from the ground I jumped off and landed on my knees. Mr. Saleri picked me up under my arms and took me inside to bandage me up.

He looked sad when I sucked in air through my teeth as he doused my hands with rubbing alcohol.

"You know, I have to tell Mr. Ford about this."

"Why, sir?"

Mr. Ford is the principal and I'm already pushing my luck with him; he doesn't want me to graduate, says I'm lucky to be back in school with only a week's suspension after the fight.

Mr. Saleri took his glasses off and rubbed his eyes. "Because Mr. Ford is my boss, because he's going to find out anyway and it's better if he finds out from me." He put his glasses back on and looked at me, his eyes magnified. "Why do you do these things, Holly?"

I shrugged. "I hear stuff, there's noise in my head, like a radio that's kinda fuzzy, and my head hurts . . . I can't explain it, something gets in me." My heart started beating faster.

He held my gauzed hands in his. He suddenly seemed old. Outside the small window in the nurse's room, the wind was blowing tornadoes of garbage around and the buzzing, the hotness, came inside my head again. I bent my hands and watched the blood seep slowly through the gauze while I spoke.

"Giselle's home and sometimes it's hard because she's kind of moody and I'm moody too but everything's OK, really, it's OK, and the fight, well, you were there, sir, the fight wasn't really my fault—I got shit for it but you know as well as I do, sir . . ."

"Don't say *shit,* Holly."

"Sorry, sir." I offer out my hand. He unwraps the bandage and takes a paper towel to wipe the fresh blood off.

I wanted to explain it more to Mr. Saleri but the words didn't come.

"There are only two weeks of school left, Holly . . . Tell you what, you make me a promise."

"What's that, sir?"

"You be a good girl, no more of this garbage, please, and I'll make sure you get out of St. Sebastian. You *and* Jen."

Mr. Saleri taped up my hand again and we both sat there looking at it, waiting for the bleeding to come through, but it didn't.

"OK."

Lunch was over, the schoolyard was empty, and there were big puffy grey clouds all over the sky. Suddenly the buzzing was gone and I could hear all the boys in Mr. Saleri's classroom yelling and whipping chalk at the board. He could hear it, too.

. . .

You can feel the cool rise up from the river even on the hottest days, that's why we go there, though the river is poisoned and there is no time. We both have places to be: Jen has to go to her sister's to babysit her nieces and I should be home studying for my math final. But, instead, we meet up by the convenience store next to school, split a grape and lime Popsicle, and walk through the park without talking.

When we get to the top of the hill, we throw our school bags down and sit there, high on the ravine, inhaling the toxic mixture of the polluted river sludge and the lilacs bursting up between the trees. I take my shoes and knee socks off and wade into the river. When the water's up to my knees, Jen lights a cigarette she stole from her sister, Joanne.

"Want one?" she yells. I shake my head as Jen coughs on her first drag and then I take a further step, trying to balance myself on the slimy moss-covered stones. I look back at Jen and she gives me a crusty smile. Her eyes are turning yellow from blue bruises, and there's a small cut on her cheek. I know it's probably not very Christian of me but I'm glad Jen has black eyes. Glad I'm not the only one with battle scars.

"I'm sorry about your face, Jen."

"Well, my mom only yelled for about half an hour and then she didn't have the heart to ground me, so I guess it worked out all right." Jen skips a rock upriver: one-two-three-four times the charm.

"Mine too. Jen?"

"Yeah?" she says, blowing out blue smoke.

"Who's he got starting next game?" I miss playing with Jen, the way our bodies find each other on the court like two crazy-in-love tango dancers, the way we can pass and defend each other blindfolded and nearly always score.

"Practice sucks without you, Hol," she says, pulling on a pair of sunglasses.

"Yeah."

"How's your sister? Still skinny?"

I nod. Jen throws a rock at my ass, then another, and starts laughing. I step back to the shore and pull myself up the hill and start pitching leaves and garbage at her. I think about how next year Jen's going to be joining all her sisters and cousins and Italian friends at high school and how I'll fit in, or not. Then Jen teaches me Italian swear words and we laugh, counting the ducks that go by.

"How come your parents never taught you Polish? Or Hungarian, or whatever you are. Manga."

Manga. Manga-cake. Only the Italians aren't mangas. I shrug and wipe my wet feet on Jen's bag. "Giselle knows a little."

"Maybe they wanted to forget, have their own secret language."

"Maybe."

. . .

When I get home Giselle is lying under a pile of blankets on the living room floor, sweating. When I touch her forehead it feels like she has a fever. She opens her blanket and I coil up next to her and whisper, "What's wrong?"

"Me," she says.

"Yeah, what's wrong with you?"

"My stomach hurts . . . I think I ate too much."

I place my hand on her slight belly and put my hand on her forehead.

"Are you OK? Should we call someone? Take you to the hospital?"

She groans, collecting herself into a ball. "No, no hospital, I think it's just cramps or something."

"You're doing so good, G., we're so proud of you."

Giselle doesn't say anything, only wipes her nose on the blanket.

I have so many things to say to her I can't even get the order straight. I want to ask her: why did you spin so far out when there isn't even that far to go in this bastard world?

At night, when the house is dark and I can't sleep, I pray for her body to grow strong. I pray for her soul to stand straight up, for the end of her nightmares. I pray even though I'm past praying. I call on Jesus though he never calls on me.

When I was stupid in my ears, when I stuffed my hands into the mouths of growling dogs because I couldn't hear, she'd grab me, just in the nick of time, always a second before the blood and tears flew.

Because Giselle put thoughts in my head and letters in my mouth when no one had the patience. She thinks I don't remember but I do, sitting on her lap, hour after hour, going over it, till I had it perfect. A B C D E . . .

It was always her voice that sounded clear when everyone else's faded or tweaked so loud I had to lock myself in the bathroom.

I uncover her face so she can get some cool air. Her skin is hot. She looks like a dishevelled angel, with the white duvet-wings folded over her shoulders. I want to tell her about this image but she says, "Everything feels like a struggle, Hol, why is that?" Her question makes me forget that my sister is a hippie-angel and then suddenly I have another picture in my head of Jesus holding his bloody, thorny heart in his hand: *Mercy.*

. . .

The next day I see my father's ghost. He's disguised as a little boy, a six-year-old wearing a striped shirt, but I can tell it's him. I recognize his baseball cap; it's the same one I saw him in at the track.

After Mom leaves for work, I'm doing the dishes when I look out the window into our yard and see him, the boy, standing there, in the middle of our overgrown lawn strewn with old dandelions. He's doing yo-yo tricks and stops every once in a while to look up at me as he winds up the string. His hat and yo-yo are both red.

He reminds me of Egg, somehow, the little kid from *Hotel New Hampshire,* the John Irving book Giselle's making me read 'cos Sol made her read it. I guess my dad and Egg do have a lot in common. They both died unexpectedly. And Egg wasn't a real person, just a character, and so sort of a ghost in my mind already, I guess.

When I finish the dishes, I hear Giselle stirring upstairs, so I dry my hands and go outside. I know he won't talk to Giselle, that he'll go away if she comes downstairs, but that he'll talk to me. As I approach him he smiles and asks me for a glass of water. I go back to the kitchen and get him one and, on the way back, I use my free hand as a machete, skimming over the grass at my knees. He giggles at this and does it himself before I hand him the water. He drinks it quickly; ghosts get thirsty too, I guess.

"Hi," I venture.

"What? Oh, hi." He continues lopping off heads of dandelions with his small child-doctor hands making *chuuuu a chuuu* noises until I ask him to show me his around-the-world again. He fits the string on my finger and shows me the proper method of flicking the yo-yo around.

"Just keep doing that," he says, stuffing his hands in his little jean pockets and *chuu chuuing* his way out of the grass and onto the pavement.

"Thanks for the water." He waves, and runs down the street pumping his little arms at his sides and making rocket explosions.

When I come inside, Giselle is stumbling around the kitchen, still half-asleep, trying to pour milk into a bowl without cereal. I put the yo-yo on the table, in front of her.

"Want some eggs?" I pull a pan onto the front element and motion to her to sit down.

"Sure, thanks." She sits there, rubbing her eyes and moaning for a while as I make breakfast.

"Why are you in such a great mood?"

"Daddy taught me yo-yo tricks," I declare, in our sunny kitchen, as my sister wakes up and looks at me queerly. The yellow yolks bubble as the new day's light blinds us both for a moment or two.

. . .

I'd really like to tell Mr. Saleri everything because I think he would understand and not drag me to some child psychologist. But there's a thunderstorm coming, and my hands are cut open, and it all seems too complicated to frame into words: my Daddy's child-ghost, not to mention Giselle's late-night fried-sardine sandwiches and how they drive Mom absolutely mental.

Still, I'd want to tell him not to worry, because you tell people, that's what you do, you explain weird stuff about yourself and your family to people who love you. Because he loved me, he loves me. Me, fucked-up little Holly Vasco. I know Mr. Saleri sticks up for me when none of the other teachers do. Thinks I'm smart but not in the normal way. Every day I twist my knees for a wing stride till it torches liquid venom on my tongue; he knows, he sees me, counts the seconds of my pace until night folds over our cold, lonely track.

And I want to tell him it's going to be OK. Because I know that he loves me, that he loves me best.

But there's a trick with me: I have to knock my head against the wall sometimes to get it to stop. Sometimes I need to jump fences, throw myself off the edge of this spinning core.

Sometimes I land so hard my head stops making its noise, then the dead go quiet, at last.

# chapter 17

Medical students will learn to obtain an accurate medical history that covers all essential aspects of history—including age, gender, socio-economic status, spirituality, disability, occupation, race, culture, and sexual orientation.

Some days it is as though I go from one madwoman to the next with only Sol in between.

Agnes and Holly are incorrigible lately.

Agnes has a preoccupation with sex, to put it mildly. It's quite unnerving; I have to dress in shapeless, baggy clothes or else she thinks I'm turning tricks when she looks away. Last week a male patient asked me for a cigarette and Agnes's eyes got all buggy, a sure sign that she's going to start in on me.

"Go on, go on and get him, I know you want to."

"Agnes, stop."

Mom's theory is that Agnes's third and final husband, Ken,

was the only man who ever loved her, or failed to beat her like the other two. But she's got to stop trying to break in to the men's rooms and calling the nurses whores, because they're getting really upset about it.

And Holly. You can't even look at her sideways without her snapping at you. She's been moping around the house ever since she went back to school. Think she might be in more trouble already.

Now, from my window, I can see her leaning lackadaisically on a rake in the backyard under the guise of helping Mom in the garden, wearing only her bra and Dad's old pyjama bottoms. She is sucking on a chicken bone, a habit she's had since childhood and that we have been unable to convince her to break. Mom is stooped under the lilac tree ripping weeds out and nattering at her.

"For God's sake, Holly, put some clothes on, what you think this is? A harem? And take that thing out of your mouth. I cook all day and then you go stealing the cat food. From now on if you eat like an animal I'm just buying Purina for you, that's it! Purina sandwich . . . ha!"

She turns to pinch Holly's butt affectionately but Holly jumps away from her and sends the rake flying into the middle of the yard.

"Don't!" she laughs as she disappears into the house.

Holly comes into my room without knocking, sits on the end of my bed, and flips through an anatomy textbook. She throws the book on the floor and slips on one of my shirts.

"I swear to God, if you get that shirt dirty I'll kill you, and please don't throw my books around. Do you know how much those things cost?"

"Relax!" she says, her face twisting into a little teenager-grimace. She extracts the bone from her mouth and holds it in her hand, looking down at it. It's shiny and grey. She does not move or say anything for a while.

"Listen, you shouldn't feel bad about the race, you can still go to basketball camp."

"I don't want to go to that stupid camp."

"Holly."

"Well, come on, it sucks. Besides——" her face softens and she stretches out next to me "——I'd rather stay home for the summer, now that you're home." She is still cupping the bone in her hand.

"What's up?"

"Nothing, I . . . nothing."

"Holly?" I run my hand through her hair instinctively. I stop, expecting her to flinch, or slap my hand away, but she does neither so I continue. She looks up at me and thrusts her jaw out as she speaks.

"What do you and Sol do?"

"What do you mean, what do we do? What are you talking about?"

"I mean, you know, what do you *do*." She turns crimson and I realize, incredulously, that she is shy.

Holly, who insists on repeating every disgusting joke she hears at school in a loud voice at dinner. Holly, who unfailingly reports to me the thwarted sexual exploits of Jen and the rest of her teenage friends. Holly, the raucous and crass creature who has always moved in her slim body with swaggering ease and immortal confidence, is shy. She is caught in her own inexperience and longing, and I am, as usual, unprepared.

I feel like laughing although I know it is absolutely forbidden. Sometimes, like now, I get the feeling that there has been some mistake, that Holly is the older one and I am the kid.

"Well, so, what do you want to know?" I say in what I hope is a sisterly way, sitting up and pulling my hand out of her hair.

"I dunno," she mumbles, the tips of her earlobes burning red.

"What it feels like, what you're supposed to do. All that stuff."

"You just act natural. When you're there, you'll know what to do. Don't sleep with anyone, Hol, you're way too young. Is there someone, someone you might . . ."

She burrows her head into her arms. "No one," she says as if she has just made a decision.

She gets up slowly, stretching as she does, recovering herself as she reinserts the bone into her mouth. I hear Mom screaming her name from the backyard.

"Coming!" she bellows, her brow wrinkling as she returns to her irritated state.

"Yeah, so thanks for nothing."

"What? What do you want from me? Hol?"

"How will I know what to do if you don't tell me?" she whines in a sudden panicky, accusing tone, before she thumps down the stairs.

Clearly I have failed Holly, and myself, in some intangible way, as I always do when she tries to confide in me. As if in my inability to transmit my experience to her, I had not lived it at all.

And all day her whiny little plea rolls around in my mind like a tuneless song that will not stop, no matter how loud I turn up the radio.

Surgical approach to the heart: Vertical sternotomy is the approach generally used.

Dear Holly:

Heart lesson #3: post-heartbreak survival.

The heart is resilient, I mean literally. When a body is burned, the heart is the last organ to oxidize. While the rest of the body can catch flame like a polyester sheet on a campfire, it takes hours to burn the heart to ash. My dear sister, a near-perfect organ! Solid, inflammable.

Heart lesson #4: the unrequited heart.

You can't make anyone love you back.

Each type of neuron responds differently and has a different threshold for excitation; they have a wide range of maximal frequencies of discharge.

After too much red wine and chocolate mousse, Sol takes me to his subterranean room. We lie on his bed kissing, our bodies shaking with anticipation and sweat. My black dress tears as he leans in and then, as we undress and he moves into me, my head gets whipped up in the familiar hot confusion of sex. It's ironic, but now one of the only times I feel connected to my body, like I am in it, is when someone touches me. When he's finally inside, he reclaims his calm.

"What do you think about, Giselle? When I'm inside you?"

"Nothing," I say, smiling. "My mind is a high blank wall."

"Mine, too."

We sleep a little, and then, as the stained blue summer morning creeps under the curtains, Sol pins my shoulders to the bed. He hovers over me, a shadow of a beard transforming his delicate face.

# chapter 18

I have an appointment with my principal, Mr. Ford, a tiny nicotine-stained man. He gets annoyed with us for our slow responses in church and spends at least an hour a week holding special school assemblies to bawl us out for not saying "Lamb of God, have Mercy on us" quickly enough.

He also has rotten teeth and meets with every single one of us eighters in his office to talk about our "High School Career," to discuss whether we are taking the right classes, etc., etc. It's pretty much an excuse for him to talk about God with us, to ensure that we will be good little Christians at St. Josephine's High next year. Besides getting suspended, and besides math, which I'm failing, I have a pretty average record. I'm no nerd, like Giselle, but I do all right. But Ford has it in for me, for some reason.

"Hello, Holly, well, that's nice of you to wear your uniform, seeing as you've missed the last two weeks of school." For some reason, this makes me laugh so I put my hand over my mouth.

"Actually, sir, I started back a couple of days ago."

"Ah yes, Carl, Mr. Saleri, mentioned something about an incident in the schoolyard at lunch the other day."

I grin at him, remembering my promise to Saleri. I need to get through this meeting, Lamb of God, please. I promise to start fresh next year. No fighting, no screwing around, no jumping off stuff (oh God) even if it means being the most stellar nerd for most of next year.

Mr. Ford looks at me with his dinosaur eyes and says, "Mr. Saleri, it seems, worries about you and that's lucky for you, Holly."

"I know." I smile weakly, watching the seconds tick away on the wall clock next to the crucifix. Then I notice a small, cheap frame of a brown-haired woman and a little boy with their arms around each other. I pick up the picture and study it.

"This your kid, sir?"

Mr. Ford gives me an irritated look but then his eyes soften. "Yes, that's Henry."

"Very cute, sir. How old is he?"

"Four, four and a half actually."

"You must be very proud."

"Yes." I put the picture back on his desk after wiping the line of dust away from the bottom of the frame.

"Sorry, sir, didn't mean to mess with your stuff."

"That's all right, Holly. Now, as I was saying, I think you've been punished sufficiently for that *incident*." He gives me a smile. How strange it must be to be so close to God and still so far.

"Well, I'm glad about that, sir, really. I'm sorry about everything that went down and I know that . . ."

He closes my folder and opens his shit-eating grin even wider. He seems to enjoy the sight of me twisting in my chair, seems to think it's funny that Mr. Saleri worries. "Well, you're a smart girl, Holly . . . some would go as far to say a little too smart to be caught brawling in the parking lot and jumping off fences."

I can't stop smiling now, it feels like my teeth might fall out of my mouth. "I know, I promise I'll be fine in high school, sir," I say, standing up and shuffling towards the door. "I mean, I wasn't the only one involved and . . ." Remember, I tell myself, no fighting, no screwing around, no . . .

"Not so fast, Holly. You see, there are some things I think we still need to discuss." He fans his palm to the chair across from his desk.

"Oh?"

"Well, to be honest, I'm a bit worried about your soul."

"My soul, sir?"

"Yes, your soul. Be seated, Holly, it's not as if you're missing class or anything like that." The nicotine smell coming from his mouth seems to get stronger, and, as if on cue, he lights a cigarette. I glance at the No Smoking sign on his office door and at the small, yellowed crucifix next to it.

"As you know, I'm the principal of this school and I take special pleasure in watching you kids grow and learn. Well, I've been watching you, Holly, for these past two years and I've really noticed something special about you."

"What's that, sir?" I have a feeling he hasn't noticed any of my wonderful hidden talents.

"Well, you're a sharp girl, as I mentioned, and you are very active in extracurricular activities and maybe this is why you think you're better than everyone else."

"What are you talking about, sir?"

"I'm talking about exactly this, Holly, the tone of your voice right now, the way you are looking at me. You have what is called an attitude problem, and I feel that it is my responsibility to let you know that in the real world, in *high school,* no one likes a show-off."

I sit up straight. My hands are drenched with sweat. I search my mind for things Ford might have seen to come to this conclusion and, coming up with nothing, I look at him straight in the eye and finally stop smiling.

"Can you just tell me what this is about, Mr. Ford? Because I really don't—"

"This is what I'm talking about, your disrespectful attitude."

We sit in silence for an uncomfortable stretch; I give up on the idea of talking. I focus instead on the half-inch ash of his cigarette and decide against telling him it's about to topple onto his tie.

"What is it about you that makes you think you're so special? I mean . . ." He pauses and flips through my folder.

I get a queasy feeling in the pit of my gut, thinking that this folder will follow me for the rest of my life, that this man, this weaselly little God-fearing man, can write things in my folder that will affect me, and my High School Career, for the Rest of My Life. But the not-snark, as Giselle calls it, the not-snark says: *Suck it up Hol. Suck it up. Don't say anything. Don't ruin this with your big fat mouth, please, Hol,* and I wrestle down the part of me that wants to scream.

"Do you think that you deserve to be treated differently, Holly?"

I say nothing.

"Can you hear me, dear? Is your hearing aid on?"

"No sir, yes sir, I hear you."

"So why, why, Holly, do I see you rolling your eyes during closing prayers? Why do you think you may waltz in a good five minutes after the rest of us have filed into class and are ready for morning prayers? Do you think you need a different set of rules?"

"No, sir."

"Do you know what happens to people that think they are special, Holly?"

"No, sir."

"They die in car crashes, in drug overdoses. You see, they never learn that they mean nothing at all. They think too much of themselves, of their worldly needs, and they don't think enough about God."

The ashen colour of his skeletal face is slightly pink, he is beginning to frighten me. I'm afraid he might have a heart attack but then he slows down, catches himself, and looks at me, sees me, for the first time.

"I have a daughter too, Holly, your age. She's at St. Mary's, so I know this is a hard time for you girls, that there are many changes happening in your mind, in your body." He gives me an almost friendly look and whispers, "I know, also, that you lost your father at a very young age, that things might be a bit more difficult for you without that guidance."

I blink at him as a single fat tear rolls out of my left eyeball and into my mouth. *That didn't happen, you didn't see that.* He looks at me as if he wants to say something else but decides against it. Then he rolls his office chair behind his desk efficiently, switching into another person entirely. He butts out the filter of the cigarette that's been smouldering in his grip for the past couple of minutes and dashes off his initials on the transcript in my folder. His hands are shaking.

"You may go now, Holly, I have other students to see."

I open the door a crack, trying, with all my energy, not to let loose the rest of the scratching wave of tears at the back of my throat.

"How is your sister?"

"Fine. Terrific."

"Tell her I say hello. Is she getting married soon? I've seen her with, what's his name, Abraham?"

"Solomon."

"Of course, Solomon, that wonderful Old Testament name . . . Anyway, goodbye, Holly, and good luck to you."

God's luck to you. The world moves in slow motion as I roll my forehead against the cool, painted, concrete-block walls of the corridor. I stay there for a while, pressing my hot cheek against the texture, breathing. Then I make my way down the calico-coloured floors of the school, looking in every now and then at everyone inside their classrooms. I hear the gummed sound of running shoes coming towards me and duck instinctively. It's Jen. She wraps her arm around my shoulders and gives me a friendly headlock.

"So, how'd it go?" Her face is close to mine and, I think, for a second, how pretty she is even with two crazy ponytails coming out the top of her head like geraniums and blue sparkles all over her face. Accessorized, Jen likes to call it.

I stare at Jen dumbly, but I don't need to talk, Jen knows exactly what happened.

"What? That crazy Ford . . . Look, don't worry about it, he gave me the same you're-going-to-burn-in-hell lecture. Once we get out of this shit-hole place, it's all new."

"Right." That wave of scratching pain-tears comes back into my throat and my mouth and it's all I can do not to cry.

"You OK?"

"Yeah, fine," I say, struggling out of her hold.

"Listen—" she snaps a yellow, fluorescent wad of bubble gum in my ear. The smell of piña colada washes over us "—I got some excellent news."

"What's that?"

Jen's got that mad-glee look in her eyes. "Listen, chickie, guess who Saleri said is starting for the final game of the season?"

"Me?"

"No, Magic Johnson, yeah you, and me, your left-hand man, Wo-man!" She gives me a big crazy smile and we start high-fiving each other and jumping up and down, until we get too loud and someone comes out of the nearest classroom.

"You ladies have to be somewhere?"

It's Mr. Saleri. He's smiling a little bit, looking pleased with himself. The shiny open pores on his nose suddenly look great. I want to kiss his pale mouth hiding underneath his little moustache. He leans against the doorway casually as Jen and I pounce on him.

"Is it true, sir? You're going to let me play?"

He clears his throat, almost shyly. "Jennifer seems to think we need you." Jen pinches me in the ass, hard.

"Ow!" I slap her hand away and she goes skipping away down the hall singing "We Are the Champions" and pushing her hands up into the air.

"But . . . um, sir, have you cleared this with Mr. Ford?"

All three of us look towards his office door.

Saleri shrugs. "Don't worry, I'll talk to him, you just make it to practice and keep doing your homework. Focus on your game." He leans back on his heels, looks into his empty classroom and then back at me.

"Hey." He sticks his hand in my hair awkwardly, like a hairdresser, trying to arrange the short little tufts in front into some kind of order.

"You OK, Holly? Something upset you?" I get the feeling like I got when my nose was broken: the snotty, teary smell of pain crunching my sinuses.

"I'm just fine, sir, thank you," I whisper, walking away from him backwards, giving him a silly little smile as he waves at me like a sad clown and goes back inside his empty classroom.

. . .

As soon as I get home from school I crawl into Giselle's bed. Her head's propped between two large books on her desk. As she reads stuff, she draws a picture of a skeleton, absently, then scrolls in the muscles alongside the bones and then, using her ruler, she makes lines coming out of different parts and writes down the names of the parts. She then draws a heart from memory and labels it quickly: left ventricle, right ventricle, aortic cavity. She does it mindlessly, the way some people doodle; Giselle's known the name of every bone and everything since forever. She's in a mood, all quiet and inside herself and has got bags under her eyes. She stares at the tiny skull Dad gave her when she was a kid. Besides her schoolbooks and her mauve silk dress, it's her most prized possession. I lie on her bed, sniffing her pillows. When she starts to shade in one area of the heart, I lean over and pull on her sleeve to get her attention.

"What are you studying for?"

"Nothing really, just reading, so I don't forget everything. What's up with you?"

So I tell her, first, the good news, about the game, about Jen and Mr. Saleri, then about Ford, his tie, his smoking, the picture of little Henry that made me almost like him. The words come out quicker and quicker till I get to the part where he tells me that I think I'm better than everyone else and the stuff about my soul and drug overdoses and people dying in fiery crashes. It all gets so mixed up in my head snot bubbles drop out of my nose while I try to explain and then I'm gasping, and Giselle sits next to me on the bed and pulls my face to her bony shoulder. I bury my eyes in her long, scratchy hair.

"Hey, hey! It's all right, Holly, shhhh . . . what an asshole."

"Ow."

"What is it?"

"My nose hurts, Giselle."

"I'm sorry, honey, don't cry, please."

"Do you think I think I'm better than everyone else?" I spit out.

"I don't know. Do you?"

I shake my head as she smooths back my hair. She holds my head in her hands, watching the tears stream down with a serious look on her face.

"I know that you are better, at a lot of things, than most people, except math."

"I don't know." I stuff a pillow over my face.

"Sometimes it sucks, being good, because if you make a mistake then everybody makes a mistake and if something goes wrong it's your fault, it falls on your shoulders. Like a bad play, you know, timing, sports has a lot to do with timing, right?"

"Yeh, yeh, yeeess . . ." I blubber.

Giselle puts a Kleenex up to my nose and says, "Blow slowly."

"Ow." A little blood comes out when I blow into the tissue. Giselle inspects the goop in my Kleenex and, without missing a beat, goes on.

"Here, take another Kleenex . . . Listen." She pulls her chair up to the bed and puts her forehead onto mine. "If your timing is good you pass the ball to Jen, right? She knows what to do, she can tell you want to steal into the key, make a layup, or shoot a hoopie, is that right?" I start laughing, sputtering liquid out from just about every orifice in my face. *Hoopie.*

"OK, sorry, I don't know all the technical terminology. My point is, I'm trying to draw an analogy here, whether you get the shot or Jen gets the shot doesn't matter. It's not just about how *you* play, Holly, it's about how you make everyone else play, too. That's why they need you."

Giselle comes on the bed and sits next to me.

"But sometimes things go wrong, you miss the shot, you get pounded in the parking lot, whatever, it's hard sometimes." She pauses. "Are you going to tell Mom about Ford?"

"I'm telling you, now."

"Holly, nothing, nothing he said was true. Do you understand me?"

I nod at Giselle and curl into a tiny ball on her bed, blowing my nose into my T-shirt.

"Ow, Gizzy, my nose hurts, my head hurts."

"I know, I'm sorry, here, take one of these." She grabs a bottle of pills from her dresser and gets a glass of water from the bathroom.

I try to control my breathing and let Giselle wipe the blood and snot from my nose and feed me pills. I feel the ache floating in my head subside and sleep coming on. Giselle peels off my runners and puts a blanket over me and I stick a piece of Kleenex up my nostril.

She lets out one of her long, slow sighs, sits back at her desk, picks up her pencil, and returns to her secret work.

# chapter 19

TB epidemiology: The wave of the European epidemic began in 1780, during the industrial revolution, and peaked in the early 1800s. By the 1960s, huge control of the disease resulted in the shifting of demographics. Eighty percent of active TB were elderly, and cases declined to about 30,000 per annum.

While Holly drools on my pillows, I read the pages of the TB chapter till my eyes are swimming. Finally, I close my book and, when I'm certain Holly's asleep, I pull out the green cloth-bound book I found among Mom's old photographs while we were housecleaning. It belongs to Dad. If Mom won't tell me the details of their escape, I'll have to find out on my own. It doesn't matter now, I don't need her co-operation, I have this new-found evidence and from it I can reconstruct the night they left. Mom thinks I can't read Hungarian but she doesn't remember Dad sitting me down and explaining phonetics, the vowels, and the consonant combinations, just like I would do with Holly, in English, several years later. Pushing my tongue to the roof of my mouth, I try pronouncing the words in my best imitation of my parents' exchanges. *Nem értem. Nagyon finom. Köszönöm szépén.* Maybe she thinks my memory of these words has been lost like this little book.

As I go through the aged, yellowed pages, I feel something strange flicker up inside me, which is what? Understanding? Proximity?

—*So what? He taught you a couple of foreign words when you were a kid. Big deal.*

—He tried.

Armed with a brand-new Hungarian–English dictionary, these last couple of nights I've been piecing together their past from my father's professional and personal notes, and their old-world documents.

—*So what?*

So what indeed. Why do I want to get into it? Why do I torture myself? If Mom's hiding something, she's probably trying to protect me. Why do I want to know about his big fat stupid heart? What possible fascination could ancient notes in a forgotten language about the blood-sugar levels of his patients and what Mom was wearing the night they escaped hold for me? His heart never did anything except keep me out when he was alive and then shut down when I was twelve. So what? Why should I care?

Because, like some dogged old detective, I am convinced that there are clues that connect us, me and Dad. Convinced there's something concrete that held him back from me. A man doesn't just wake up one morning and stop loving his daughter, just like that, his flesh and blood, his—

—*Why do you always have to push? Why can't you just accept that you hated each other's guts?*

—Because it's not supposed to be that way.

Because now I don't need her, or his ghost. I only need his heart's words, and tonight seems as good a night as any to take on the challenge of the group therapy assignment to write about our families. So, after a lot of pacing, looking up words in the dictionary, and trying to pronounce their foreign textures in my mouth, eating half a rotten apple from the bottom of Holly's school bag, smoking a cigarette, and writing three ragged drafts, this is what I come up with:

## The Story of Your Flight

On this balmy June night in 1971, outside a small village in northwestern Hungary, Thomas takes Vesla by the arm, detects the flush of excitement from the surge of Chanel perfume off her neck, one of Misha's last gifts to his young bride-to-be, he thinks. He reaches into his jacket pocket for his notebook and the pile of cash. After a little research, he's discovered that rather than getting fake passports, it's more practical to arrive at the border without any documents. He has burned their passports, along with all evidence of their identities: they've become untraceable. He is buying their freedom and has already destroyed their past.

Reaching for the thick wad of cash—money he has carefully collected over the years—he withdraws it from his right breast pocket. There's the fruit money: saved from summers when he was fifteen and plucked chalk-blue plums and pink peaches from trees on his uncle's fields. Factory money: the mindless two-year stint where he greased and moulded mysterious bits of heavy metal together in a village with a population of five hundred, when oil clotted under his nails like black seaweed stuck on a shoreline. Finally, the greatest dividend: the blood money. After endless intern nights at the country's largest city hospital, where he did not sleep for three years, he conceded, taking up a friend's offer of easy hours tending to the medical problems of ranking party members.

He slips the money, the years of his past life stacked and accounted for, into Vesla's pocket; it will be safer with her. He wonders, as he does almost every day of his life, about his decision not to join the party.

Years later, in Canada, in the mid-1970s, colleagues, friends, strangers at dinner parties will peer at him curiously and ask, "Why did you leave?" He will smile back at them, pulling his lip self-consciously over his yellowed bottom teeth, while running his tongue over the top stack of his brand-new dentures. He will take a sip of his cocktail and smile at these British descendants, who recall only black-and-white images of smartly dressed women holding guns during the Hungarian revolution, and a paprikas recipe, but who have no context, not really. Nobody has thought about his country since the October Revolution, since the newsreel images showed Russian tanks rolling over cobbled streets. He will try to explain that success, in medicine, in academics, in any field, was reserved only for those with Communist connections, with money, or those willing to become good Communists. He will try to explain but the words will fail to come. Misha's name will not rise to his lips. He will not ever say the words "murder" or "suicide" out loud. Instead, he will run his tongue over his smooth teeth and say, "Economic reasons."

He knew politics intimately enough, he saw their bile clogging the arteries of the men he treated. Rich food, drink, and cigarettes: the occupational hazards of powerful men. He measured their political clout according to their too-high heart rates, and, listening to their fat hearts in their fat chests, he heard the echo of a thousand unknown stresses; this was the sound of manifestos, the great levelling of class. At night he tempered the clang of their heartbeats by assisting at an illegal abortion clinic. As he cleaned the women and pulled sheets over their hips, he noticed their collective silence and how the undetected burst of a heart flame quelled offset the wild hearts that pounded out his days. And one day he woke up and thought, "This is not me, this is not my life. My life is somewhere else."

All of those heartbeats, like the pile of cash in the pocket of Vesla's green dress, added up to this unfathomable future moment of his life which was now here.

He slips his hand into the pocket of her coat for one lingering moment of stillness. Then, at once, in his temples, he hears the racing stethoscope crash of sick thunder, babies screaming, a woman's groan.

A sliver of pain sluices his own heart, paralyzing him for an instant. *This is what it must feel like to die underwater.* He pulls his hand away from her side, presses it over his heart. It feels as hard as thick glass. Confused, he knocks his knuckles against the weight of his glass heart, which, he realizes now, is the half-full bottle of vodka in his pocket that he drained before meeting her.

The stillness gone, Thomas and Vesla walk out from the sanatorium, arm in arm. The pain has travelled to his stomach, lancing it in criss-cross patterns. They've only got to walk through the mountains and surrender at the border. It's simple: they state their purpose, stay in the camp, and then apply to Canada. They won't refuse a doctor and a nurse; he's heard Canada wants professionals.

The large doors wheeze closed and he thinks of his failure to protect Misha. Misha, young, healthy as a mule, who, despite this, complained of headaches, staring spells. Thomas wrote his diagnosis and recommendation in his journal, in his steady, doctor's hand: *Prone to seizures. Order tests.* But his mind snaps closed, like a camera shutter. He hears the click in his head and turns to her.

She smiles grimly and walks fast so her thick-soled shoes

do not sink into the dirt. He looks at her as she tugs him along like a sleepy child and he is gripped by her determination to get through things, to run. He thinks of her slowly expanding body beneath her snug green dress, about the child arriving in four short months, about his impending fatherhood, the way her sleep has become deeper, the way she laces her fingers through his at night and pulls him close. He thinks of how surprised he was to see her on the steps of the sanatorium, three weeks ago, with a single suitcase and a handful of wild-flowers.

When they get to the edge of the forest he takes out his compass and checks. "West, right? We're going northwest."

West like the pictures he has seen in books in the city. West like cowboys, like James Dean's hair falling loosely. Fields cluttered with trees, and wheat, and lakes, and farms. Thin white British ladies poking their pinkies up to the sky, teacups flying into the air like tiny gold-plated spaceships. North like chimneys, fleshy polar-bear skins. West like Indian feathers swaying in a dance. North like moccasins and beads sewn in the sun of August and worn in the damp of winter. North, where the colour is red and white and brown and yellow; how sepia can disappear when you travel, when you move.

They start to run blind; he's now dragging her as they clop their hooves over leaves. They run on, waking animals, becoming animals. She is screaming at him:

"What are you doing!? We don't have to run, Thomas, stop it!"

But he is running into another country. He is confused, thinking if he can keep going, keep pushing, keep dragging her along, they won't even notice, they can run right to France and then leap right over the ocean like in fairy tales. He can jump over the ocean, with a woman in his arms.

He runs right up against a large Austrian officer who catches him and tackles him to the ground.

He lowers his head and surrenders, to what, he isn't sure.

"It is part of the plan," he says.

"What plan?!" she screams. "There is no plan. Oh you, you've read too many books." Then she begs him to be quiet. "I'm sorry, Officer," she says in perfect German. "My husband has been under a lot of stress lately, he's a bit confused, we've come from the hospital, we have our papers here." She hands over two-thirds of Thomas's life savings in a ripped brown envelope and smiles at the guard confidently. "I'm sure you'll find everything is in order."

Thomas considers his one-day sons, how they will never wear uniforms, will never have to bribe those in authority or compromise themselves. Then he is sick, the combination of anxiety and alcohol too much for his weak heart and gut.

(He does not know yet that he will have no sons, that the only thing he passes on from this journey to me, his daughter, will be the tiny dry skull of a monkey, and the fragments of this story I am now pooling together through the scant resources he left me from that old life, from his journal with some of his medical papers folded into it. Also, there's a photograph of a young man, which I slip between a folded sheet of paper; I am not ready for this piece of evidence yet. I cannot look.)

He then holds his hands above his head and feels the cool earth below enveloping his knees. He vomits, his belly sour and betrayed. Afterwards he feels better than he has in years, vanquished, forgiven, done with. The heartbeats fade out, leaving his mind quiet and still.

*I have come a long way to prostrate myself before a stranger,* he thinks.

He was thirty-one, shit-scared, lonely, and sick with hope, my proud, fat-hearted father: an immigrant, at last.

# chapter 20

That night I sleep on Giselle's bed and get woken up in the middle of the night because of Tammy's barking. Tammy, a small annoying beagle, is the neighbour's dog. Mom is yelling at Giselle not to go out. When I get to the top of the stairs I see Giselle's wearing her Walkman, she's got the keys to the car, and she's shouting at Mom through the loud music coming out of her big earphones.

"Why are you always pushing me?!" Mom yells, wrapping her robe around herself and trying to get between Giselle and the door, saying "Shuuuuuu, shut up you. Tammy-dog!" through the screen door. Mom yells something to Giselle in Hungarian and looks up at me helplessly, as if I could stop Giselle from doing anything she wanted to.

"What's going on?" I go downstairs and let Tammy in. I bend down and the little dog licks my face, wagging her tail, excited to be part of this human nocturnal drama.

"Shut up, will you?" says Giselle, no lover of animals, as she kicks past both of us and wedges the door open. She turns to me and says, "One day we have to sit down with a good psychiatrist, like a real one, with two PhDs, and sort out all the lies in this family."

"Like which one?" I ask, standing up next to Mom.

"Ask her. Ask her yourself."

"OK," Mom says, pulling Giselle into the living room. "I'm telling you. I'm telling you everything now."

I can hear Mom's voice trying to calm Giselle down while Tammy clamours against the screen door. Part of me wants to listen to Mom, to find out what the hell is going on, but I can't move. Ten minutes later Giselle rushes by me and slams the door. Mom stands behind me and we watch as a furious Giselle revs the engine and squeals out of the driveway and down the street.

. . .

Giselle and Dad never got along so well, it's true. Now Giselle's on a mission to figure out why, or to punish Mom for their relationship, or I don't know what. But they weren't always at each other's throats. Maybe Giselle can only remember the bad stuff, but I remember some breaks from their tug-of-war screaming matches.

The summer before our father died the whole family took a trip to Europe. I must have been about four, Giselle eleven. I have a funny memory, which feels more like a dream, of Europe being grey and dirty and all of us staying in a small hotel room and Dad yelling at us to stop jumping on the springless bed.

What I do remember is Yugoslavia, which is no longer Yugoslavia now, I guess, because of the war.

Our parents took us to Split, where they had friends who owned a huge rundown hotel by the seashore. Every morning Giselle and I would put on our bikini bottoms and run into the sea and let the salt water strip our skin dry. Afterwards, we'd sit with our legs sprawled in the water and ogle breasts; it shocked and pleased us that Europeans strutted around half-naked.

That was the first time I saw a man naked and, that same summer, Giselle tried to teach me how to swim. I remember spending hours and hours wearing those floaty wings and pad-dling, uselessly, between Giselle and whatever grown-up she had enlisted for the job. I never did learn how to swim prop-erly, and the ordeal usually ended up with me crying and Giselle splashing water in my face and leaping into the water mermaid-style. She would swim away from me to do her long ocean laps alone.

Despite the swimming, Giselle and I got along very well and so did Giselle and Dad. Instead of fighting they simply ignored each other. The only time he didn't ignore Giselle was when she was swimming. He'd follow her out and tread water no more than ten feet away from her every time she went out. If Giselle noticed this, or cared, she never let on.

The grown-ups, our parents and the loud big-boned German couple, our parents' friends, were unpredictable. Now that I think about it, they were probably drunk most of the time. They spoke, it seemed to me, about eight different languages and it was usually hard to get their attention. But as soon as we realized that we were unwanted, we did just fine.

Our days were usually devoted to tormenting the small, strange salt-water tadpoles and trying to make fishing poles out of whatever bits of string and branches we could find.

Our day would be interrupted only by grown-ups shoving bottles of Coke and salami and paprika sandwiches into our hands. Sometimes we would shake Dad's pants out and collect the dinars that fell from the pocket to go down to the beach store to buy ice cream. If it was raining, we'd play hide-and-seek in the cold hotel rooms, or put each other in the dumb-waiter, then run to the upper floor and hoist it up.

I copied everything Giselle did in those days; I wore what

she wore, said what she said, and did what she did. At home it was a constant sore point, but for those three weeks by the seashore it didn't seem to bother Giselle that I had to wear my matching sundress when she did, that I repeated every foreign word that she had somehow picked up. It didn't bother her that I wanted to hold her hand. She combed my hair out and smoothed out my dress as if I were her favourite doll, before we walked down the path to the beach.

At night we fell into our shared bed exhausted and happy, listening to our parents' strange and mysterious languages float up from the stone terrace lit with tiny white Christmas lights, where the two couples sat at night, after dinner, drinking and talking and smoking.

And Giselle and I weren't the only ones in love. Peeking out of our hotel room on a rare night when I could not sleep, I saw my father jump up from the table of conversation, trying to distract my mother from the German woman's loud laughter. Giselle pushed her arms onto the sill, to watch the adults, to watch our silly, drunken father.

He was tanned and had a cigarette clenched in his mouth. He was wearing a clean white shirt that was unbuttoned halfway to expose his tanned chest. His dark hair was parted on the left side. He pulled my mother into a dance, and, as they moved to the gypsy echo of the music coming in clearly from the nearby seaside restaurant, the Germans were quiet for once. I had a flash of panic: things were too right, too peaceful, too calm. *Something terrible was going to happen.* We held our breath, watching them in that muted half-beat moment, while the sea lapped quietly and the music died low, and then we sighed out together, into that huge, impossible cavity of dread.

# chapter 21

Students will be versed in knowledge of appropriate statistical methods to test cause-effect relationships.

I shake the car keys in my mother's sleeping face.

"I need to know who my father was . . . I need to know *now*."

She jolts awake.

"Tell me about him, because I cannot imagine it anymore, it makes me mental. Tell me, or I'm leaving this house right now and turning you over to Children's Aid. I'll take Holly, marry Sol, and you'll never see us again."

"You are talking nonsense. You know who your father was." Mom's face goes blue in the half-light, but she looks relieved somehow too.

"No I don't." I hold up the cloth-book.

"Where did you find that?"

"Never mind, I found it."

She tries to grab it but I end up flinging it across the room and all the papers fall out and scatter in the darkness.

## Vesla's Story

She sits slightly apart from the after-lunch, summer-house crowd. She looks out at the river. Between her narrow hips, her small belly is swollen. As she pulls her hand, replete with engagement band, over the thin cotton of her dress she is filled with the twin impulses of terror and ecstasy. The women grow quiet as boisterous male laughter barrels out onto the veranda, and when she looks up, the women have all grown silent, watching her through half-closed eyes. And then one of them rises from her chair.

"Someone's arrived."

The main door cranks closed and announces the newest member of the river party.

"It's Thomas."

She hooks her head back to better hear his movements. The women's eyes are all wide open now and crosswords are dropped, nail-polish bottles are recapped, the sleepy post-lunch ease broken by a squeaking door and the young doctor's arrival.

"Was he even invited?" the standing woman asks Vesla as they collectively slide their eyes to the interior of the cottage. Vesla doesn't answer, she is praying that he cannot see her profile. She pulls her mouth into a grimace so that even if he does see her he may not recognize her for the ugly expression on her face. But Thomas doesn't notice her, he is speaking in soft tones to the servant who is offering him vodka, coffee, dumplings, and a cold-meat plate perhaps, sir? She hears him decline, place his doctor's bag on the table, and make his way to the smoky backroom. The laughing stops and everyone listens as a gust of wind slits through the high branches of the trees surrounding the summer house.

Everyone can hear Thomas ask to speak to Misha, privately. A series of tests, the results of which must be discussed, so sorry to interrupt but it is important; *sürgős,* urgent, Thomas says, using the Hungarian word reserved for emergencies, a word that ignites meaning at the top of the lungs brought to the front of the mouth like a swift kick to the throat, a word that he knows politicians will respect and defer to. Misha excuses himself and leads Thomas to a small shed at the side of the house that the men have set up for a poker game later that night. Inside is one hanging light bulb, a card table, and five chairs.

Vesla wonders what it might feel like to get out of her chair and walk straight into the Danube, to feel the warm water at the top of her neck and the icy pull below at her feet, to walk to the middle and, after one last breath, submerge her head. She imagines herself doing it, the shouts from the shore, the wooden doors of the shed banging open, Misha and Thomas united, at last, by the source of their problems being dragged southward, to the bottom of the Aegean Sea.

The women decide to change into their bathing suits and walk down to the shore, a colourful group of hats, chaises, beach bags, and brown legs. One of the younger ones offers a hand to Vesla but she shakes her head and remains rooted, her head pulled towards the shed, which remains quiet.

Twenty minutes later, as the women are almost completely assembled on the thin strip of dusty beach, the rest of the men snap the elastics over their fat, hairy stomachs and pound out of the house like teenagers, running together into the river. The women scream and laugh and spit sand out of their mouths.

Amid the chatter at the shore, the shed door opens and

slams. She turns to see a white hand fly out of the shed and another hand slap it away. Misha shoulders up against the door; he hooks on the latch and locks it. He strides up the veranda, his heavy Slav jaw set in anger, his features suddenly frightening.

He kneels next to her, looking out at the others, taking her hand and clutching it so tight she fears he might break her fingers against the ring.

"Tell me it's mine, Ves."

"It is, of course it is," she lies, not knowing the answer.

Misha rises, his face arranged now, the shadows falling like old leaves sliding off rocks in a heavy rain. Then he goes into the house and five minutes later his dark, lean body folds into the river and he swims as far into the middle as he can. She picks up a cold, greasy drumstick and walks to the shore, pulling her hat over her ears, deaf to the screaming coming from the locked shed.

Students will learn the ethics of medicine: Knowledge of beneficence, non-maleficence, autonomy, consent, confidentiality, disclosure, justice.

—*It's a talent, really, honey, to be able to come up with at least half a dozen things that depress the hell out of you at any given time.*

—Then it is a very great talent that I possess.

Four hours after hearing Mom's story, I'm sitting in a twenty-four-hour barbecued chicken restaurant drinking coffee and waiting for Sol, trying not to stare at the lump of potatoes on the plates on the table next to mine and not to think about what they would taste like mixed up with sour cream and butter, thinking, I can't stop feeling as though everything around me is buzzing, is defiantly real, despite the fact that it seems as if it's a dream, is not true if none of it's true. The only way to keep my skull from swelling and exploding, to keep myself from falling into this darkness, is to cling to real objects: a spoon, a chicken carcass, the cigarette shaking in my hand, mashed potatoes, the clock. Because all there is is the empirical; if everything you've based your life on is not, naught. Not if your father isn't your father at all, not if what you've been told is a lie, lie, lies.

And I have proof, photo evidence to be filed away. But I haven't looked at Misha's photo yet. It leaped out of the book, fell face down, on the floor. I've only read the inscription in my mother's handwriting on the back: "Misha Kovacs, 1971." Because there is a possibility that if I see his eyes, the cut of his face and jaw, I will understand everything.

Sol arrives just as I order us an entire chicken dinner with all the fixin's and a potent Portuguese wine.

—*Why do you love people who never love you back?*

"Oh, I thought maybe you were standing me up," I smirk as Sol slides into the booth across from me.

There it goes again, her negativity, the self-saboteur always ready to pipe up and drive people away, but I'm wanting to talk to Sol. I need him to tell me that he loves me, that I'm not a terrible person, daughter, girlfriend, that I deserve the truth. I try to block out her voice that loves to attack anyone who gets close to me. I want to fill the space between goodbyes and hellos with mindless, idle chatter, mundane mashed potatoes, anything. Words may protect me; that was the whole idea of group, right? Saying it out loud, purging ugly thoughts.

"I asked her, I asked Vesla who my father was."

Sol looks at me carefully and wipes his black, inked hands on the napkin and pours himself a glass of wine. He is silent, waiting for my explosion of anger or tears but they don't come. Instead, I hold out the photo like a hardened cop on television enumerating mutilations on a murdered body.

"This is him, this is Misha."

Sol takes the photo and lights a cigarette nervously. He looks at the photo, then back at me, then back at the photo, comparing.

"Vesla told me he died swimming in the Danube after Thomas gave him some bad news about his health, but she swears I'm Thomas's."

"But you don't believe her?"

I shrug and take one of Sol's cigarettes. "She says she saw me and just *knew* I wasn't Misha's."

Sol bites the side of his cheek and pours himself more wine. The waiters begin singing a song in Portuguese, low and timbersome; their voices fill me with the sadness of crying too long and the sea.

I peer over at the photo.

"Have you looked at this picture yet, G.?"

I shake my head. "Can't. Not yet. Why?"

It seems to me that everything will be made clear by this new piece of evidence, but, judging by Sol's head-scratching and looks, suddenly I'm not sure at all.

—*There is, of course, the possibility that you are not a bastard child.*

And if, for all those years, Thomas hated me because he thought I was not his, what then? His love, precious and accounted for, could not be squandered on me because of questions neither he nor I could answer. Thomas couldn't ask the question of science that mattered, simply couldn't ask that of her, directly. Well, if you are roaming in your semi-ghost life tonight, Thomas, at all curious if your decision to dismiss me was warranted, stay tuned, because this is the moment we can settle the matter.

"What is it, Sol?"

Sol bites his lip. "Well, just for the record, I have personally always thought that you look like Holly and your mom."

"What're you saying?"

He drops the photo under the table and, climbing for it, his voice rises from under the formica table-top. "Let's just say, your mother had a type."

For the condition called "high cardiac output failure" the problem is often not the failure of the pumping ability of the heart but instead the overloading of the organ with too much venous return.

When Sol sleeps, which isn't often, his dreams are a thousand running streams that never find each other. They never form a lake, or even a puddle. I know he is sometimes afraid to fall asleep, that he stays up and watches me for a long time, like tonight, when he's worried about something. Lately this something is me.

Tonight I take a sleeping pill and offer Sol one but he refuses: Sol, who'll ingest endless amounts of whisky, ibuprofen, and coffee, often in combination, despite my doctorly advice against this practice, is oddly purist about sleep: either it comes or it doesn't. After all the food and excitement, I can't handle being awake anymore, so we have long, slow, lingering sex, both of us committed to forgetting the events of the night or at least pushing ourselves to the limits of exhaustion to part with it. Afterwards, we finally fall asleep, or at least I do. I've never really seen him resting peacefully. I always fall asleep before him and wake up after him. Once or twice I've seen him with his head buried under his arm, but when I looked into his quiet little arm-place he peered out at me, eyes open, lashes fluttering. Mostly, like tonight, we stay up too late talking and making love to sleep.

Sol is also superstitious; he thinks of himself as powerful. Take, for example, his idea of streetlights going off when he walks by them. "Didja see that?" he'll say when a dim orange light pops off as we pass it. And I never have the heart to tell him that lights flare on and off when I walk down the street, too, that wild, staring animals come up to me bearing gifts of gnawed bones and other such mythic messages. Maybe his not sleeping does make him powerful, makes him see things, understand the logic of random power surges and wild animals. Maybe it's what allows him to write about accidents caused by slothful hands, murders committed in the deep swollen night. But then maybe he's just a teenage insomniac who needs a cup of warm milk.

Once I talked to him about how Holly sees Dad at track meets and stuff but it didn't seem to faze him.

"She sees him out and about in the world. Like he's a normal person?" he'd asked, more like he was confirming something than being purely concerned.

"Yeah, she says she does, I mean who knows?"

He shrugged and slid his eyes away.

"What, Sol?"

"Nothing . . . I just don't think you should get your undies in a bunch worrying about it too much. I don't think it's a problem, that's all. People see stuff."

—*You'll never keep him, he'll leave, just like all the others, he'll* . . .

—Shut it, just shut it today, all right?

In the morning, I curl my fingers up under the hot blasts of water in the shower, and then dress, gulp down a cup of instant that Sol calls coffee, and find that I feel better, all cried out and dried out. At least, I can begin to figure out how to rid myself of the troublesome hum of her off-key voice, even if everything's just become more confusing than clear. That's it, I feel like I'm beginning, that I can finally learn to be—

—*Happy!? You tear your family apart and you're happy!?*

—Since when have you cared about my family?

This shuts her up. I run outside, pull on my sunglasses through my still-wet hair. Sol's waiting for me in the car. When

I get in, he slips his hand between my crossed legs and drags on a cigarette, filling the already balloon-warm air with smoke, and adjusts the rearview. At the light, he leans over and kisses me. "You look like . . ."

"What? Who do I look like?"

"You look like your sister today."

"Impossible. Could we not talk about her right now?"

"All right, sorry, it's just, I've never seen you in that sweat-shirt before."

"This is my goddamn sweatshirt, see." I pull up my shirt, flashing Sol. He laughs, relieved that I'm making a joke of it.

The city is stiff, still rising from a long summer night of heat, emerging from its exhausted air-conditioned gloom. The street sweepers leave a mist of condensation that we follow.

He parks the car and we walk across the wide field between the parking lot and the hospital. Sol tries to do cartwheels on the wide lawns, but he's not nearly as good a gymnast as Holly and always ends up on his ass. As we enter the grim, green geriatric ward hallway through a side door, a fat man, wearing an unbuttoned shirt and heel-worn slippers, shuffles down the corridor and gives us a crooked, delirious grin. Sol grins back. I think about how strange it is that I am on the inside, the sane side, of the hospital doors. I've spent my short adult life now on both sides, as med student and patient; a safety to others but a danger to myself.

We stand outside the thick, steel institution doors of Agnes's unit. I see Agnes through the small circular window, waiting for me. She is clutching a little gold purse and wearing her usual suspicious frown and wild-blue eye makeup.

—*She'll make him. Make him love her.*

"You OK?"

I nod.

He pulls me to him and I smell his singular, neutral, dusty-boy-wood smell, and wave to Agnes over his shoulder.

"Goodbye, Gizzy, watch out for those crazy ladies." Turning on his heel, he walks down the hall, whistling quietly, raising his elbows against the early-morning mental-hospital sun. He says something but it gets lost in the crash of meal trays down the hall.

"What?" I turn towards him.

"Later," he says, pointing towards the future. Then, walking quickly, he makes his escape.

That afternoon, after work, I read in the library for a couple of hours, then I walk by the café where Sol and I are supposed to meet. I see him through the window, smoking a cigarette and doing a crossword puzzle, waiting for me, but I don't go in. Instead, I go home, return the car. No one's home so I take out Mom's scale and weigh myself, note that I've gained four pounds since the fight and the chicken-breakfast extravaganza. Promising to starve myself tomorrow, I go out again and walk through the low orange-lit streets, where only skater-punks and people turning off their sprinklers are about. I sit down on a wide curb and watch the end of the summer-night sky fade into that odd bruised-purple colour, and suddenly I feel completely paralyzed. I'm not used to this, having someone waiting for me, having someone (could it be?) *love* me. And I'd be lying if I said I didn't remember the touch-and-go terror of love Eve inspired in me. That's another terrible thing about love; once you've had it, you cannot go back to not having it. The only way I knew to live without love was to not eat, study, and try to push Eve, and all she meant, back to the farthest quarter of my mind and it had been that way ever since, ever since—

—*Abandon or be abandoned. The rules of engagement are simple.*

A sweat breaks out all over my body, the uncontrollable wash of perspiration you get right before you throw up.

—*He's going to mess everything up.*

And I realize she's right. Sol won't mess things up, literally, like with me and him, but with me and *her*. If I let him in, I let her out. Her scrupulous control of my food intake, of what I do and say, will have to disappear, eventually. That's what relationships are, aren't they? The compromise of self for another. I realize that what I have perceived as safe is dangerous. Hadn't it been that way with Eve? The slight curve of Eve's belly, the warmth of her nipple, the perfect rhythm of our steps on asphalt, the way our bodies fit so well in sleep, was all so deceptively harmonious because, in reality, we were hellbent and raw, and even our quiet moments together seemed dangerous and transient.

—*Love fades, doesn't it?*

I pull a floppy cigarette out of my pocket and think: isn't this what I've worked for all these long weeks at the clinic, to break up the tedium of controlled days, to free myself from her simpering cruelty, her flat slaps across my face? But how can I open myself to Sol when something in me clings to the comfort of regimentation, to being marked and checked by an impossible taskmaster who is bent on diminishing me to a tiny shred of marrow; when I was at my thinnest, no one could hurt me.

And yet there's the heart-shaped twist of his mouth when he tells a joke, his curly hair, his slim delicate brows that make him look actorish, dramatic. There's the way he looks at me sometimes when he thinks I don't notice, like he's making a promise or praying.

Sol is different. He's not Eve, he's not Thomas, he's himself. And what is it in the unique Solness of his being that has me believing in the possibility that love might make us all better people? Perhaps Sol will quit drinking so much, start sleeping more, I'll gain a few pounds, we'll look less marked by life, less haggard. Or perhaps we won't change at all, I don't know.

—*That's it! You don't know. People's feelings change. Daily.*

But it's impossible to explain anything; everything with her has to be concrete. We have to rely on our ability to pounce and leap and survive on the lean picked-over hunt of others. Still, she has grown oddly quiet, listening for once.

I walk back to the house through the grey streets. Inside houses, TVs are being turned on. They cast a blue light in living rooms. The day is cooling off, the sidewalks smell like bubble gum and fresh-cut grass, and I feel safe in this weird suburban world, surrounded by shiny foreign cars and ridiculous dwarf lawn ornaments; if I wanted to, I'd never have to leave here.

But she just can't let me enjoy it, she just can't let me ride this delusion up the cracked tar driveway that Thomas had paved the last time in the 1970s, instructing the whole operation in a pair of lilac jogging pants.

Then the words jut out the side of her mouth, involuntarily, like a badly hidden smoker's cough.

—*Just remember, love is always betrayal for you.*

# chapter 22

I sit by the sprinkler, peeling the skin off my feet before putting my socks on. Sol drives up. I scratch at my aching ribs, but it's the pleasurable pain of healing. I tie my shoes tightly. Sol gets out of the car and stands over me.

"Going for a run?"

"Yup."

"Where's your sister?"

"Dunno."

He takes off his sunglasses and looks down the street as if he expects Giselle to materialize from the quiet suburban lawns. His dishevelled profile leans into his own long summer shadow and he looks doubtful for a second, lost.

"Do you mind if I join you?"

"You need shoes, you can't run in those." He looks down at his dusty boots.

"Wait."

I go into the house and find Dad's favourite tennis shoes buried under a heap of boots, newspapers, and umbrellas. Stan Smiths.

When I come out of the house, Sol is spraying some kids with the sprinkler. I hold out the shoes. He smells like sandal-wood oil.

"No arch support, but it's better than nothing."

"Thanks, Holly. Listen, she didn't call or anything? We were supposed to meet after work . . ."

I shake my head and, watching him bending over to tie his shoelaces, I want to touch his hair.

"Shouldn't you be at school?" Sol's eyebrows pull together.

I shrug, "Last day."

"Oh." Sol frowns mildly as he stretches his legs.

He sprints out in front of me, leaping over ditches, confident in dead man's shoes. I move behind him, counting the steps between us, planning on catching up but pacing myself because I want to run long, until time is measured by pavement, empty streets, and identical houses, learned by rote. And I am thinking *Today is the Last Day of School and I am, as usual, not there.* And I am thinking, I am sending her a secret telegraph to plug up her ears.

. . .

We move like moonlight on waves. We trip through the tennis court, Sol tangling himself in the net on purpose.

"Jesus, stop! I need a break!"

I cartwheel on the doubles lines as moths fly up into the pink fluorescent light and a middle-aged couple on the adjacent court can't decide whether to laugh or be annoyed with us. Moths explode into dusty puffs, the dust on their wings floats into the white air as the couple tries to figure out the score:

"Thirty-love or forty?"

Sol's flushed and sweaty. He jumps over the net and runs out of the court.

"Race you to the DQ. Loser pays."

"You're on." And I'm off, an easy stretch ahead of him, the length of a sleeping whale, dreaming of soft-serve and yellow out-of-bound balls.

. . .

When we get home it's dark in the house. Sol opens all the kitchen windows and starts going through the cupboards searching for dinner.

"Hey, your mom ever go shopping? How does canned clam chowder with crackers sound, Hol?"

"Great." He turns on the radio, which is playing jazz.

"So, how you feeling these days? Get into any scraps lately?" He watches my face to see if he can smile. I let him.

"Yeah, well, they're used to sending us Vasco girls home. When Gizzy was seven they sent her home with a note that said Mom should comb her hair. I got sent home once for not wearing underwear." I shrug, Sol stirs the soup, and the kitchen becomes filled with the sound of his light laughter. *He is a man,* I think. *There is a man here with me.* Then I feel weird about saying "underwear" out loud.

I empty a vase of foul-smelling flowers into the sink. We reach for the tap at the same time. Our hands collide for a moment before his fingers make a small bracelet around my wrist.

I drop the half-filled vase, which he catches, then he pours water over my head, still laughing. I turn the tap up and, with my one free hand, splash him with water. He is laughing and shrieking, letting me, but he is not releasing my hand, *he is not releasing it.* Then he slips his wrist into my palm as if we are playing a private game of shadowing. The other hand flutters like a dim, quiet bird on my hip and scales the length of my wet shirt, uncertainly, as if it doesn't know whether to fly away or land. He lets go so my arms can wind themselves over his shoulders, where I feel how strong he is; how little it would take for me to buckle under him and open.

I am a clean fine bow and Sol a slim, fine arrow, diving. In my throat, the dry echo of unthinking; where we have run, and who has left us behind while we were racing. And the salt that runs from our eyes is not sweat that he is lapping up with his hair but, like blood, it's me and my name that he says, over and over, in our kitchen, me that he is touching with his mouth, on my forehead and my cheek and my neck. Just then, the sound of the front door closing rips us apart. And our moments get broken apart by our leaping, my fleeing into the wooden chair on the other side of the kitchen and the sudden panic in his face as he leans his hips into the counter.

Giselle walks into the kitchen and tosses her bag into the corner. This is what she sees when she turns to look at us: me, panting and soaked in the corner, and Sol, gazing above her head, clumsily arranging bowls and spoons with his hands that were birds and now only guilty weapons.

"Hey, beautiful." He flicks water at her and she looks straight into his eyes, which are slippery coals now.

"This is cozy. Water sports?"

"Where you been?"

"Oh, you know. Out and about. Actually, I went to the library to study."

"You sure?"

"Yeah, I'm sure."

"I thought we had a date."

"Sorry." Giselle's mouth twists into a wicked grimace.

"You hungry?"

"No."

She darts a look my way that is so practiced I turn away from her and concentrate, instead, on my shedding feet. There is a moment, just one, of peaceful silence, of believing that Giselle has not caught us at anything at all. But then it passes.

Giselle looks at the water on the floor and at the two of us, her face wrinkling, knowing, not guessing, but knowing.

"So, where were you?" Sol presses.

"That's not nearly as interesting as what you guys were up to, I'm sure."

"Just tell me where you were, Gizzy." His prodding, which is worse than his own lying, turns me cold.

"I know she's deaf, but are you? I *told* you, I was at the library."

Her smile is a cold spasm of pain and all of her anger and knowing cuts into him. I want to stand in the line of her fire to deflect it. So that she will know we were one together and not two, caught, for a second, in one cage. But, before I can get between them, Giselle presses her hands to her forehead and lets out a low moan.

"What the FUCK, Sol!!!" She leaps on his back.

He drops the spoon he has been clutching. His face shuts down. He walks down the hall with Giselle hanging off him, still screaming. I grab her shirt to stop her raised arms that have begun to rain blows on the back of his head. I pull her from him because he is not protecting himself, he is not resisting but letting her, like he let me enter him in heat, he lets us take him over.

"Eat your goddamn soup!" she screams, dragging me back to the kitchen on the frayed tail of her shirt, before hitting the pot into the sink with a wide swoop of her arm and burning us both.

. . .

I'm sorry, I am, because you're right, Giselle, we don't need to share everything. But the next time you come leaping at me, I'll be ready. The next time you come swaying your fucking bag of bones and burdens, I go straight for the jugular.

Straight to the teeth.

# chapter 23

Stab wounds of the heart usually cause rapidly increasing tamponade.

*Love is not popular anymore. It is thankless. Noble. Do not expect any reward. Trust yourself.* Someone has penned this on the bathroom wall in the bar, and, every time I pull my head up from the toilet between spitting and retching, I see it. After throwing Sol out of the house and Holly into the sink, I go to a downtown bar and drink martinis till the oily, salty flesh of green olives and alcohol brine is all I can taste.

And I stay there, past the post-dinner crowd, until closing time. I try to make meaning out of those words as I excise every last piece of food and venom I contain. And then, with the razor-sharp sentimentality of the wretchedly drunk, I get it, and that stranger's bathroom philosophy becomes part of me, as surely as the scar on Holly's forehead is part of her.

Once upon a time, on a hot summer day, our father cried,

"Look at the sun!" and our mother, just out of the car, neatly plopped Holly on the concrete—on her head. That moment left a scar extending from her hairline to her left ear.

—*The thing you were most careful with, you lost.*

The sun, not to mention the moon, hung like huge globes of malleable fire in the great northern sky that day. Dad was right, it was stunning, but Holly didn't look so good.

So, here I am, in a downtown bathroom stall thinking about that well-stitched line on my sister's head, about the scars I want to put on Sol's head as those words stare down at me: *Love is not popular. Not noble . . . not love, no reward. Trust love. Is not love. Trust yourself.*

I try to put it all into some kind of order, to measure memory, betrayal, to get the stories straight, thinking that, maybe by putting her story next to mine, I can get close to Sol, understand him. Because he loves her, too, he is part of my story and hers.

My parents scraped Holly off the ground and she was happily sucking on an orange slush an hour later in emergency. I remain on the toilet-stall floor until the memory of that moon-sun day and all the booze have given me such a colossal headache that I can't think about anything anymore, especially the rapid contusions of love. Then I pass out and dream of cords plugged to my face like leeches, my arms strapped down, electricity jolting through my palms. When I wake, a piece of sharp green glass on the floor is cutting into my hand and I know it's a sign. I etch a letter on my hand; put it on top so I can see the jagged edges bleeding out: *S*.

S is for sorrow, for all I don't say. S is for sick now, my punishing ways.

Remember, an ounce of prevention is worth a pound of cure: avoid "misadventures" with sharps.

*—Hello, My Name Is. You. You. Giselle. Me. She.*

What is betrayal? What is betrayal, split in two? What is betrayal? Is what, betrayed by you. (Again.)

*—Betrayals are measured by what is offered and what is taken up. Goddammit you're stupid, didn't you learn this already?*

The heart forgets what the body remembers. As I try to get up off the bathroom floor she shoulders her way up to my face and screams insults.

*—You expected him to love you?*

She taps me on the shoulder, my hungry, doubting companion. She's always with me, like a jealous streak, a trick knee, a weak stomach, a bad heart, this hunger is DNA you cannot undo.

Like fleas, or the smell of cheap cologne, she is hard to get rid of. Smiling, smug, arms crossed, her pixie-toes tap out a metal rhythm that sounds like the smack of surgical tools falling onto a metal tray. Like genius or sorrow she has curled up inside me and censors no evil, no criticism.

*—Get up off the ground, loser.*

Sometimes she's British. Sometimes she is a poet. Sometimes she has a drawling southern accent when she mocks me. Other times she is long-nailed and pure JAP. She's got a rough cat's tongue and a debutante smile. She's got a Chanel bag, can outdrink me any day, and is the skinniest girl I know. But she is always, always right.

*—I want you to curse every time you stole a kiss from his cheek and thought you knew love.*

She likes to skip around and wear transparent Victorian nightgowns even on the coldest nights, in order to mock my shivering mortality.

Occasionally, late at night, she is kind: she lights my cigarettes, pours me drinks, and waits quietly for some mutual banter to emerge.

*—You're a real piece of work, you know that?*

—I know.

—*And that sister of yours . . .*

—I don't want to talk about her.

But more and more, she resembles a lion-woman: her hungry iron gaze is trained on me, never wavering. Her eyes penetrate; she is always prepared, always ready to pounce on the slightest vulnerability. When I stumble on the street she laughs: proof. But when I slip into my clothes, and they hang a little looser, she pats my back and hands me an extra sweater, my lion self.

She is incomplete, a succubus: trigger-happy, toilet-mouthed, knife-wielding, blue and white and sometimes green in the face from screaming, from telling me all I cannot have. When I manage to beat her down, tie her into a chair on the far side of the room, get her to eat some food, she smiles her sanguine, toothless grin. She starves proudly, waits, like a saint, she waits for death by fire or baptism.

—*This is when,* she spits, when it is three o'clock in the morning and I can't sleep from hunger.

She is holy, wholly my own, and when I reach out to touch her image in my face, she hovers an inch or so before my skull. Then she flicks her tongue out at me like the enraged lion she is; she snaps my fingers between her feline jaws; a barrage of dead spiders, splinters of wood, and bone.

—*This is when I love you most.*

No new method and no new discovery can overcome the difficulties that attend the wound of the heart.

In group today, after everyone commented on how I looked like shit, we were supposed to read our little essays about our families but I'd forgotten mine, so when my turn came I said,

"My dad died a long time ago." Then I told them about the time Dad tried to teach me gymnastics.

Before that, all the girls had been complaining about their dads. Things were going "the Sylvia Plath way," as Susan used to say. Walking out into the summer night, I heard Susan's high-pitched Scottish voice in my head and laughed out loud: "My father had such high expectations of me, my father wanted me to be the perfect little girl, blah, blah, fucking blah. If every woman adores a fascist, it's her own fault."

She claimed Sylvia Plath was the patron saint of anorexics and Electra-complexed women everywhere, but I've always sort of liked her poetry. It's not often that you read someone's words, and their pain, which has been dead for decades, lives on to give you a headache. I think there's something to be said for that.

I told the group about how, one day, Thomas seemed fixed on the idea that I should learn the perfect cartwheel. The fact that I was a chubby uncoordinated child who preferred reading to gymnastics did not faze him. We were on the front lawn and I could barely hold up my weight each time I did the turn. When I was upside down in the air, he held my legs.

"Straight!"

"Ow! Daddy!"

"Straighter!"

Then Holly came along. Holly, who could run before she could speak, Holly who could throw a baseball hard and fast and long; who'd had the perfect backhand by age seven, who didn't have to be taught a thing about the physical world.

She couldn't get enough of him, and she lunged at his legs when he came in the door. He was the magnet she crawled to when she could not walk and, when she could, his hands were the pinnacle of comfort. In my memories, she is always stroking them, kissing them, somehow attached to them. They seemed, to my mother and I, twin beings, this man and his child.

But it would be fair to say that Holly's "disabilities" were counteracted by my growing brain, as our father's disdain for fat and lazy women was rivalled only by his condemnation of stupid people.

Before he started growling at me for touching his things, before the screaming and fighting became the holding pattern of our relationship, I used to tug the instruments out of his pockets as she shimmied up his back and rolled over his shoulders when he came home from work. So certainly, together, we made the perfect daughter. Together, it seems, Holly and I can share almost any man.

part ii

# chapter 24

Shock or angioplasty is required immediately to reinstate a stopped rhythm.

"You can't wear black to your grade-eight graduation!" Mom says.

"Why not? You wore black to Aunt Judy's wedding."

"That was different."

"Why?"

"I was in mourning. Stop moving, Holly, or I'll stick a pin in your leg."

Vesla has Holly in a silken, raglike dress, with a floral print. She is trying to figure out how to take the waist in so that Holly's torso will be vaguely visible.

"Why don't you let her wear my dress?" I hang on to the edge of the doorway, framing the question in a mild voice. Feeling weak, I sit down on the laundry hamper to stop my sudden swooning. This is the first time I've acknowledged Holly since the fight. She shoots me a grateful look.

"OK."

Mom gets up and spits the pins out of her mouth; a gesture of letting the operation go.

Holly rips the dress off as she skips out of the room.

"Thank God she's graduating."

"Of course she is, she only missed a week of school."

Holly clears her throat from the hallway.

"Do you have shoes?" I yell.

"Oh! Shoes." We hear her darting into my room. When she finally gets my shoes on, she slides into the room campily. I catcall and Mom lets out a surprised laugh. The long, tight, black dress is cut up the length of her left leg. She kisses the air, swivels her hip, and then, sucking in her cheekbones, struts up and down the hall.

"Holly, you're a fox. Really, you are," I say, laughing, thinking about how Agnes would react to the dress.

"Too much." Mom shakes her head. And as Holly plucks a carnation out of a vase and places it in her mouth, Mom turns to me.

"Is Sol coming to Holly's graduation?"

His name that has not been spoken, that we have not said in weeks. Neither of us. And now hearing it out loud, we both turn to look at the sound of his name, like a car crash between us.

Failed hearts: Experienced cardiologists are able to assess organ damage immediately.

—*I told you so.*

Causality. The law of cause and effect. What are the reasons? But there is no order. No who or what. No direct factors leading up to the disappearance of my body either, though the lion-queen believes she has all the answers:

—*Funny that.*

—What?

—*How all the men in your life leave you for Holly.*

Medicine was once a clean, easy, causal science to me: identify the symptoms, locate pain, perform bloodwork, analyze urine, take X-rays, then add it up, listen to your patient, proceed with a differential diagnosis. This is how I came to medicine, why I preferred it over psychology. This is why I wanted to fix broken bodies, not broken minds.

You can never get to a person's mind. You cannot know the different deeds and missions of happiness; you can't tell a scream of pleasure from one of pain. Sometimes, we can barely read pain. Neither a barometer nor a guide, pain can mislead us. Even in the body, the laws of chain reactions can be false. This is why people always want a second opinion.

It is important to appreciate that the lessening of pain does not necessarily indicate the underlying condition has been resolved.

Walking around the well-tended grass at the graveyard, I think maybe I should become a pathologist. Mom pats the earth gently, making a little lump around the new orange tiger lily she's planted at the base of Thomas's grave. She stays on her knees for a little while, wiping the stone with a handkerchief, pulling weeds up from the earth, making order.

Holly hates "the stone," as she calls it, explaining, "That's not him, that's just the place where they put his body."

"I know, but what else are we supposed to do, Hol?" We have this conversation every month, when it's time to go to church and visit the stone. "It's for Mom, not for him, or for you, it's not for the dead, the dead don't care." Holly usually starts to throw her clothes on the floor at this point in the conversation and complain that she has nothing to wear.

But I like the stone, it helps me keep things straight. The last time I saw him he gasped like an animal whose limbs were being severed. After we came home from the hospital, my mother stared straight through us while Holly and I sat in front of her, mini-zombies, staring right back. I think of awful wayward things: the heart-disease corpses we used to dissect in school, their bulging arteries and veins, and then I think maybe becoming a pathologist isn't such a great idea after all.

I know Holly talks to him and sees him and has this real spiritual connection and everything, but it's different for me. I like to preserve the image I see in the odd seventies photos of a handsome, grinning man with sharp cheekbones and polyester collars. In photos his image can't wander, he can't become someone else.

My mind is an ugly place and I can let almost anything go to rot in there. And anyway, what would I say if he strolled up to me, like he does to Holly? What in the world would I say? The sad thing is, I've imagined that too. I know exactly what I'd say if my father came up to me in broad daylight, offering me some of his ghostly advice. I wouldn't even let him talk. No.

*So what? You remain the fucking ghost you always were to me,* I'd say, and then I'd walk away.

Cervical dilation to allow an easier passage of menstrual blood in patients with severe degrees of dysmenorrhea may be helpful in rare instances but is not generally recommended as routine.

I saw her today, on my way to the library, on an escalator in the university. As soon as she saw me, I turned and started running the wrong way down the escalator, excusing myself and bumping into people. But she caught up to me, as she always does.

*—What're you doing?*

I felt the bottoms of my feet lighting up, on fire. I crashed through people, plastic bags split open, and books fell onto the metallic teeth of the stairs.

"Watch it!"

*—Why can't you see that I'm all you have?*

She comes to me, quietly, calm-before-the-storm serious, when she knows I can't run. In the middle of the night, when I'm standing in the kitchen, trying to fill the gnawing gap in my stomach, she marches right up and starts her lecture:

*—Just go to bed, you don't need food.*

—But I do, I'm hungry.

*—We don't get hungry.*

"We do get hungry," I say out loud to a yogourt container and a soggy bag of french fries Holly's left in the fridge. "People get hungry and then they need to eat," I say loudly, trying to drown her out, stuffing Holly's old fries, the yogourt, a block of cheese, and a piece of bread into my mouth, all at once. A plate of cookies, a hunk of steak from two nights ago, down, down, down, as she gets louder and louder.

*—But you'll be different when you finish, you'll be fat.*

She marches me into the bathroom and unties my robe to reveal my proud little swollen belly.

*—Good Lord, look at yourself.*

—I'm looking.

I see it protrude over my belt, the soft fold of skin, no longer concave and hard. I trace my fingers over it and think of how Sol used to like to rest his head there and read the paper. I try to reason with her.

—People eat. They eat and work and love. That's what they do, that's what I do.

*—Not you. Not us, we are stripped clean of want, we move like lean lions, we do not gorge, like you just did . . .*

*—But . . .*

*—But nothing, ow. What's that?*

Something hot and wet and foreign in my crotch. I strip down, find I am leaking.

*—Blood.*

—Yes, blood, my first period in three years.

*—Goddamn you!*

I kneel on the floor naked, blood snaking under me, warm and vile on the clean white floor. *Dysmenorrhea: the cessation of menstruation.*

The cessation of the cessation, the end of the end. She yanks my head over the toilet bowl and knocks it against the rim. I encircle my growling stomach.

*—You'll clean yourself up and starve that away, young lady.*

—I will not.

My stomach feels distended. It knots as she grips me, shoves her fingers in my throat till all I've gulped is gone down, down, down the bowl.

*—It's been a while since we pulled that old trick out of the bag, eh?*

—Yeah.

I flush and scrub the toilet, the floor. Then I run water in the tub and lower my body into the scalding heat, see my skin go pink when it touches the water. As the steam rises I place my hands over my no longer inflated belly and rest my head on the edge of the tub.

*—You're so pathetic . . .*

—I did what you wanted, just leave me alone now, please go.

Her jaws open, I insert my head between the shiny incisors, rest my head on her warm tongue before blackout—teeth crashing down on my skull.

*—You knew it'd end up like this. I go when you go. That's the problem, don't you see?*

# chapter 25

I'm playing pick-up with some older guys at the schoolyard when Roy yells, "Time out. Hey, Holly! Your boyfriend's here." And when I turn to see what they're laughing about, I see him, his arms stretching over the diamond-shaped spaces between the metal on the fence. And I'm embarrassed for him, looking so diminished somehow by the large grey fence that separates us. I take my bandana off my head and retie it as I walk towards him. I hear the tinny sound of the basketball reverberate in my head and feel the guys' eyes follow me to the fence. I aim my own eyes above the hill, beyond him, so I do not catch a glimpse of his beauty or worry.

"Hi, Sol."

"Hi."

"There's nothing to say, there's nothing."

"I know, but I can't sleep, not even a couple of hours anymore and my eyes were hurting from not seeing your sister or you."

"I don't care! You never sleep! Jesus, you come here to tell me your eyes are hurting?"

I don't want to think about his damn eyes. I don't want to talk about them even though he is wearing the sunglasses Giselle bought for him and I couldn't see his eyes if I wanted to. I remember him mock-complaining that the glasses were too dark. But he was impressed by her gift, I could tell.

"How is she?"

"She's OK . . ." I pause, and then decide that, despite everything, Sol deserves to know the truth. "Actually, she hasn't got out of bed for a week."

"She sick?"

"Yeah, sick. Listen, I gotta go, we're losing." I kick at a pile of gravel. One of the rocks bounces off Sol's knee.

"OK. Sorry, Hol," he says, dismissing me. I look at him, open and shamed. Then he says something funny in a quiet voice, almost a whisper.

"This one time we were walking in the park and there was a plastic bag on the ground with a cherry pie in it. She scooped it up as if she just left it there and forgot about it and we walked some more and then sat down on a little hill. She ate that whole pie. Didn't say, 'Gee, that's weird finding a pie on the ground' or anything, just opened it up like she bought it herself, and ate the whole damn thing. No fork. No spoon, nothing. Just broke the crust with her fingers and started in. Didn't even offer me some. Not that I wanted any. I don't like sweets. And I hate cherry-flavoured anything. . . ." He pauses, kicks some more gravel, and then lights a cigarette and sighs.

"I think about her all the time. Can you at least tell her that?" he asks, stuffing his hands in his pockets. As he turns and makes his way back up the hill, part of me is running around the fence clinging to his side and not walking back to the court.

And that part of my heart, which is tangled and blurred and pawing at his back, is not breaking at all. My sister's heart is not breaking either. I swear I didn't break it when I held it in my hands again.

. . .

The next day is Sunday and Mom and I spend an hour and a half pulling Giselle out of bed and trying to make her look presentable for church.

"You promised me," Mom says through fuming, closed teeth, while yanking clothes off Giselle's floor.

"What?"

"You promised me this bullshit was over, Giselle." Mom grabs Giselle's arm and clutches it to demonstrate how thin she has become. Giselle whips around with surprising strength, snatches the clothes out of Mom's other hand, and throws them on her bed.

"Leave it!" she shrieks, hysterical suddenly, tearing herself away from Mom's grip.

At breakfast Giselle eats a piece of toast, an orange, and a soft-boiled egg, then says to Mom, "Happy?"

"Do I look happy, Giselle? I'm putting you back in clinic if you keep losing weight."

Giselle looks up at Mom, her eyes big, scared.

"No."

"Yes."

"You can't do that, I'm an adult."

"Really? Do adults have to be badgered to eat properly? Do you know any adults that need to be constantly monitored?"

Giselle gives Mom an icy look and snatches the last piece of toast from the plate.

"OK."

"No, I'm serious, this isn't a game, look at yourself. You look like—" Mom says, pulling on her summer coat.

"All right! I get it. I'm eating, I'm eating!" Giselle yells, tears welling up in her eyes as she tries to swallow the dry piece of toast as fast as she can.

By the time we get to church, Giselle looks almost normal although her hair is still matted and puffy at the back like a guinea pig's and her tanned stick-arms are poking out of the blue dress Sol bought her when they first started dating, but she looks better than she's looked all week. It's the first time she's left the house in a while.

Mom likes to go to church about once a month. "For your father," she says, though he never came with us when he was alive. He liked to spend Sundays, instead, in his pyjamas, reading the paper and then, later, if it was nice out, puttering around all day in the garden, by himself.

We all stand straight but Giselle's got the side of her hip pressed against mine and she's pinching me with her long slender fingers, pulling at my skirt, trying to make me laugh or scream out in pain. "Stop it!" I hiss, arching my back even straighter. "I said *stop!*" Mom gives me a dirty look.

When the priest finally settles into his sermon, Giselle collapses on the pew like a drama queen and starts picking old pistachio nuts from the bottom of her Sunday purse. She opens an old tube of lipstick and collects the fluff from the bottom of her bag between her fingers. After prying a closed pistachio nut open, she offers me the green nut by pushing it onto my lap. Mom stares straight ahead, ignoring her. I pick up the nut and chew it slowly, as the priest's voice takes me far away from our small neighbourhood church.

I think about my dream last night where Giselle covered me with leaves and then snaked her hands through the musty-smelling pile. In the forest we saw giant blue swallows, the size of watermelons, and bees so heavy with pollen they looked like they were about to burst, but instead they floated harmlessly through the air and smiled at us with cartoon faces.

*God, I don't know you, only in feelings like that dream. Dear God, I try to pray but I always get distracted. Dear God, please help us, keep us three together,* I think, falling down slowly in my head, in a pile of red and brown leaves with Giselle. *God? Should I tell her about seeing Sol? What he said?*

The priest is talking about the time Jesus threw all those blasphemous people out of the temple and how MuchMusic and TV are kind of like those merchants in the house of God. I open my eyes, see Giselle with her mouth open, slouched over the pew. She looks thin today, too thin to hold up her long body in that blue dress. Giselle wraps her coat around herself, though the church is humid. I meet Mom's eyes. *She's getting worse,* her worried look transmits. I promise myself to take Giselle to the park for a picnic tomorrow. Giselle's eyes wander over the Stations of the Cross—her favourite thing about church. She stares at Jesus' Fall. Poor old Jesus, lugging that cross around, falling all over the place and everyone trying to talk to him at once. Then Giselle kneels down before the pew, before it's time to, and clasps her hands together like some pious little girl—her second favourite part of Church: looking pious.

I try to get back into my prayer, so I close my eyes. See, this is what always happens, I get lost, too lost in the world to concentrate on believing, too caught up in counting Christ's ribs or Giselle's ribs or worrying about my shoelaces breaking before Friday's game.

*Dear God, forgive my sloth. Dear God I can't talk right now because Giselle is poking me with her pointy little finger again and laughing into her hands.*

· · ·

Giselle comes into my room at night when she can't sleep. Lately she's been on this quest to find out about Dad from me, as if I know something she doesn't, even though she was older when he died. She picks up objects from my dresser: a piggy bank, a sweat sock, a St. Sebastian ballpoint pen with a picture of a flying eagle on it. She contemplates each item and rolls it around in her hand before putting it back in place.

She sits on my bed and pulls the curtains open a bit to look outside. Then she tugs my ankles into her cool palms and massages them gently.

When it is late and I am half inside the womb of sleep, ready to part with the day, why, why is she so full of questions? She wants me to tell her.

"Explain it to me."

"What?" I shift in my pretend-sleep.

"Why do you get to see Dad and I don't."

"I can't," I mumble.

"It's because he loves you more, isn't it?" She shakes my arm. Then she hides her face in her hands, says, "I keep dreaming he's trying to do something to me. He straps me down on a hospital bed with all these wires, and attaches this machine to me. Like he's trying to electrocute me. Like he's trying to—" She opens her eyes wide and stops talking.

"Nobody's trying to kill you, silly, it's just a dream," I say. *Nobody. Except you.*

"I didn't say that he was trying to kill me," she says slowly, turning to face me.

"I know, it's just that, well, you made it sound like that."

"He would never do anything to hurt me, right, Hol?"

"Right," I say, holding her tired body up against the fading shadows of the room. "Never."

# chapter 26

Many patients coming to surgery have associated nutritional disorders.

Something evil is happening to my stomach. That's the only word for it. It has turned in upon itself like an animal beaten for so many years. Sheets soaked, cramps all the way up to my neck. The pain is bright and hot and numbing, fomenting in the centre of my womb. The blood flows out of me like waves of loose ribbons.

—*This is the part . . .*

Shhhhh, I say. For once I'm the strong one. The pain ebbs and I feel myself rising.

—*This is the part where everyone says "I love you" and pretends they mean it.*

# chapter 27

Every day I watch her frame shudder at the sight of food and the blue veins take root in her face. I watch her fade. Watch her eyes grow darker.

Mom prepares Giselle's breakfast tray in the early morning. On it is a large plate of eggs, tomatoes, cheese, jam, toast, yogurt, and a steaming cup of coffee laced with brandy and cream. She stirs sour cream into the yogourt to make it richer, and adds an extra pat of butter on each slice of toast to sneak in calories where she can; she's been reduced to tricking Giselle this way. I watch her silently, eating a piece of cheese, and when I take the tray from her hands she says, "No, I'll do it."

"Please, let me, Mommy, let me talk to her."

Mom's hands clutch at the tray and then let go. A fat tear rolls out of one of her golden-brown eyes as she turns back to the sink.

Giselle's sitting up in bed looking particularly white under her slight tan, as if she's been up all night. I sit next to her and braid her dreads. She groans and picks at her eggs, and, after getting her to take a couple of bites, a sip of coffee, some of the yogurt sour-cream concoction, and a couple of spoonfuls of jam, I give up.

I roll her over, sit on her back, push my hands into her spine, and start massaging her gently.

"So many people love you, Giselle, so why can't you, just a little?"

I close my eyes and start to rub her neck, but then I feel something wet and I look down at the bed and there's chocolate-coloured blood soaking the sheets, the blankets around Giselle's waist, everything, soaked in it.

"Holy shit, Giselle."

I leap off her and run to the door, my pyjamas covered with her dark blood. "Call 911," she says without even lifting her head to watch me go.

. . .

After settling Giselle in the back seat of the car, I sit up front and I sneak peeks at Mom, thinking, for the first time, that she looks older. Mom's hands are shaking as she puts them on the steering wheel. The lines round her eyes and lips are creased and her hair is floppy and grey where it used to be full and auburn. I think about a beautiful photo of my parents that I found tucked in an old cloth-book in Giselle's bag that fell out (I swear) when I was sorting her stuff out for laundry. *Vesla and Thomas, Canada,* it says on the back, in my mother's proper right-leaning handwriting. There were all these letters and official-looking yellowed papers in another language. I tucked them all away into a white pillowcase. I'll bring it to Giselle later, maybe, if she asks for it, or else maybe I'll keep the picture for myself.

The photo looks like it was taken at Niagara Falls. Dad's wearing his long brown coat, his hair is short, fifties-style, although it's the seventies. *Papa, why are you always decades behind and still manage to look so good?* Mom's wearing a red and black polka-dot dress, with a big sash across the front of her stomach, and is holding her large belly. New immigrants, happy and exhausted, and a little proud, too.

*Giselle, we will name her Giselle, after no one's mother.*

*What if it's a boy?*

*It's a girl, I know it is.*

The falls are hazy white in the background; Mom and Dad are squinting from the spray, the sun. They are leaning together on the rail and she's tired and striking, in an exotic heavy-lidded way. Looking at Thomas in that picture, I get a funny feeling like I drank too much water and it can't make its way down the pipes of my stomach properly. It's nothing, or almost nothing, the emptiness in the back of his eyes despite their happiness. It's nothing.

I turn around to look at Giselle in the back seat as she opens her eyes to see the blood blooming in swatches on her blanket. Her pupils widen, they look so huge in her small white face. Then I remember how Giselle is one of those people who can't wait for things to be over, even fun things, like concerts, or camping. I'm afraid she might just tear through her life without ever enjoying anything, except this, except pain. Still, Giselle's misery is terrible and beautiful, like stained white cotton dresses.

# chapter 28

Intra-peritoneal haemorrhage results in a huge internal bleed which reveals the importance of taking menstrual/sexual history into account when examining females of reproductive age.

"Intravenous! You're on intravenous?" Sol says, pinching the tube lightly.

The last time I was in the hospital being fed by a tube it kind of freaked me out, but it doesn't anymore. People act all shocked about it, so I blink my eyes at them and manage a sick little smile but, really, the idea of having something hooked up to me has lost its novelty.

Sol looks penitent, and I mean to reassure him, but when I try to whisper I discover there's a tube in my mouth making speech impossible. He brings his face close to mine. I can see the hairs in his beard growing in, covering the smooth white texture of his clear skin. His breath is warm and his lips feel soft on my brow.

"We're going to get through this," he says in his whispering way, like the time we hit a cat on the highway and drove it to the nearest vet and Sol sighed all the way while it lay dying in the back seat. He takes my hand gently and I fall into sleep before I can wonder at those tears, wonder at these new ones now.

The occasional case of endometriosis produces such intense symptoms in a woman who wishes to maintain childbearing potential that bowel or bladder resection is necessary.

It's August, 5:00 a.m., the first summer without Dad and the three of us are trying to sleep in Mom's bed. The heat from the floorboards is rising up and floating over me in hot unending waves, barely dispelled by the fan mixing up the air. From the hallway, I hear Holly's child-feet beating out an uneven patter on the floor.

*Thump, thump, bwaa.*

*Thump, thump, bwaa.*

Of course, Holly's deaf in one ear; half the world is muted to her, so she doesn't even know she's waking us up. Mom groans and rises, calling to her.

"Holly!"

*Thump thump thump thump bwaa.*

I pull a pillow over my head; the cool material is soothing for almost ten seconds before it becomes suffocating.

"Shut up!" I scream, throwing the pillow towards Holly's little silhouette, which has appeared in the doorway.

With the heat wave has come a contagion of lice that has swept the grade-one class. Holly's head has been shaved completely. She ducks my pillow and rubs her hand over her little-old-man head. Then the click of her turning her hearing aid on. Ah.

She tap dances for a moment, lifting up the bottom of the long cotton nightshirt she has decided to wear for this evening's performance. I growl at her but collapse on Mom's lap, too hot to pursue my attack. Our bodies stick together in the shallow air.

Mom yawns, and runs a hand through my long hair. "What are you doing, honey?"

Holly talks out the side of her mouth, like she's trying to be a wise guy: "Hopscotch."

"Oh, you're being a very funny-guy! You're coming back to bed now," Mom says, and, as if coaxing the cat from under the porch, she pats the place beside her.

"OK, but first! A puppet show!"

Holly yammers with her hands in mouth shapes, an incomprehensible mesh of gibberish and cackling and high-pitched titters.

I look at Mom.

"Listen to me, I'm being very serious now, come back to bed or be quiet."

Holly stops and jumps on the bed, tearing off her nightdress. She sits before us, cross-legged, her arms folded against her flat, naked chest.

"Mama," she says seriously, her head shining in the night, tilting towards the fan's breeze.

"What's a *Black Widow*?"

She turns the volume up in anticipation of the answer.

---

The nature of pelvic pain caused by endometriosis is variable. Minimal endome in the cul-de-sac is generally much more painful than a huge endometrium within the ovary that is expanding freely into the abdominal cavity.

Every night at the hospital it is the same dream: everything is quiet. I am in a small hole in the earth. A young man finds me in the forest under the wet, mossy rocks. I'm wrapped in pink butcher paper, the kind that's waxy on the inside. I'm sleeping and there's something sticky in my hand.

The man unwraps me and holds me to him. I'm the thing he finds to keep, me. My bony knees ache, *growing pains*, I think.

He walks, holding me like a baby, though I'm too big to be a baby. I am a child's size but light enough for him to carry with one hand swinging free so he can pick up snails, suck them out. Salty and slippery, the snails flow down his throat like hot shots of moist liquor.

The sky is partially blocked out by him, so I can't see his face. There is something between us, something I need to tell him, but I still can't see his face.

*I have your hands. See them? They are yours. You can have them back if you want, I will give them to you and go without hands because I would like to have you back in this world, if that is at all possible. I have your legs, your shoulders. You can have those, too, if you need them. Your face I'll keep for myself, let no one see. It is the one thing of ours I will be selfish about, and no, you can't have that back.*

*That is your punishment for dying, for leaving me alone with all these strangers. You will be known as the man without a face—it will always belong to me. I am you. And you are mine, so you can't already be gone.*

We walk into night not forming words or thoughts, just watching the dark map of browns, greens, and blacks turn the night over, like erosion. *You make me feel like I'm in another country,* I want to say, but I fall back into sleep within my dream, into the crook of his arm, lulled by his steady, strong heartbeat.

Then I hear the first break, the crackle of dry leaves and stones pounding together; he lets go and I fall down on top of a rock. I stumble, my knee raw and scratched. The throaty ache of a scream rides up my throat, but this time, when I open my eyes, I see him walking ahead. I clutch at the mass in my hand and open it: nothing but pulp and blood.

I reel up and feel electrodes attached to my spine, forehead, and neck, inside my face. Black straps hold my body in place on a stretcher as a gentle current of light passes through my body.

This is not a dream now but memory. Me, trying to open my mouth, to ask why, and when will it stop? Suddenly, Thomas's face floats up in front of me, unconnected, just a head. He looks down at me curiously as he pumps me full of white burnt light.

# chapter 29

I'm just back from visiting Giselle at the hospital and I'm sitting on the porch watching the neighbourhood kids riding their bikes up and down the street when Jen comes skateboarding down the block.

She tips her skateboard up and shoves it under her arm. "You're coming tonight, right?"

At the end of the year, there's always a creek party where all the kids from St. Sebastian go to drink beer with the kids from the high school until the sun comes up.

"Marco's going to be there, come on, Holly, I know you like him."

"So?"

She sighs. "Look, go tell your mom you're going to go with me. Better yet, I'll tell her." Jen pounds up the steps to my house and yells, "Mrs. Vasco!" until Mom appears at the top of the stairs.

"Oh, hi, Jennifer, nice to see you."

"Mrs. Vasco, it's OK if I steal Holly away tonight, right? It's the graduation dance and all."

"Holly, why didn't you say anything?" Mom comes down the steps to give Jen a hug. Mom loves Jen, she thinks she's "feisty."

"What will you wear?"

"I could wear my black dress."

"No black dress. See, that's why I'm here, Mrs. Vasco. I'm giving her a makeover at my house. My sister's a hairstylist," she adds, as if this fact clinches the whole deal. Mom looks at me as I shake my head. "Well, let me give you some money to take a cab home after the dance, Holly."

"Can she sleep over at my house tonight?"

"I can't. I have to go see Giselle at the hospital tomorrow."

"No, it's okay, you go with Jennifer. I can go alone."

"Are you sure, Mom?"

"As long as it's all right with Jennifer's mother."

"Sure, sure," Jen licks her lips and rolls off in front of me on her skateboard as I grip Mom's arm for a second before tripping down the porch steps in my untied shoes.

Jen's house isn't quiet like ours. She has one of those great houses with lots of traffic, food, and activity. I always like going there for dinner and lunch and hanging out with all Jen's cousins and sisters.

"Hey kid, want some pesto?" Mrs. Marinelli asks, blowing me a kiss from the stove as a bunch of kids pull on her apron, begging for ice cream money.

"We're getting ready for the dance!" Jen announces as she drags me through the basil-smelling kitchen and into her sister's room.

Joanne was in Giselle's class in high school, they used to be friends. Giselle likes Joanne but always refers to her as "that incorrigible gina." Joanne's spread out the contents of her makeup bag and laid out her curling iron and all her hair products in front of the vanity mirror. The whole thing is making me really nervous, but Jen even has a solution for that, because when I sit down in front of the vanity, she pours us each a glass of her father's homemade wine and proposes a toast.

"To playing basketball next year!"

"To getting out of St. Sebastian!" I offer.

"To looking beautiful," Joanne purrs, slicking my hair down with pink hair gel.

"So, let's have another glass of vino and then we'll head to the creek."

"We're not going to the dance?"

"No, wiener, we're not going. It's almost over anyway, but we *are* going to the creek party."

"So why am I wearing all this crap if we're not going?"

Jen grins at me, showing off her wine-stained teeth as she pats down her stiff, hairsprayed hair, trying to undo the damage of her sister's curling iron.

"Quit whining, you look fantastic, Marco's going to be all over you. Besides, at least you don't have big hair."

I start giggling as Jen groans. She does have big hair, and no amount of patting down or rearranging can shrink it.

"You mess with that style, Jen, and that's the last time I do your hair!" Joanne shouts from the bathroom, insulted.

"You buzzed?" Jen asks, pulling a baseball cap on and throwing herself down next to me, among all the clothes and makeup on her bed.

"My face feels red. Is this drunk?"

"It's close. I'm bringing another bottle down to the creek."

"Won't your dad miss it?"

"Naw, he has so much booze he doesn't even know what to do with it."

I sit up and stretch, feeling the soft edges of the world bend around me. Everything feels like it could be funny or far away or sad. This must be drunk, too.

We shoot down the stairs screaming our goodbyes. I grab Jen's hand and run as fast as I can till there's grass underfoot.

Till we hit the park and jump down the dark ravine. Till we smell the smoke of a medium-sized bonfire lighting up the corner of the forest, where people have gathered and have started drinking in the last shadows of the day. Till we walk right into the warm wind of summer and feel it, lifting up our arms, till I almost forget about Giselle biting down on the doctor's hand with her half-rotted teeth.

. . .

Trashed. Jen is trashed, I think, as I watch her laughing, bending like a rubber toy at her waist and spilling wine onto the ground. Jen introduces everyone swiftly: "Holly, that's Clive, this is John, my cousin . . . he's just here for some junior-high tail."

There are about fifty people in all, mostly older kids, from high school. Someone's parked a beat-up old car in the ravine, opened all the doors, and cranked up the radio. Aerosmith. No graduation would be complete without it, Giselle tells me later.

"Marco's here!" Jen slurs, jabbing a finger into the air before it falls on my shoulder. "Go talk to him!"

I look over to where the tall, long-lashed Marco is standing. He's watching the fire intently, surrounded by older high-school guys. What Jen hasn't noticed, though, is that he's wearing a white shirt and dark dress pants, and that Kat, dressed to the height of virginal fashion, is standing next to him. They've come together from the dance, and Kat's even wearing a white orchid corsage pinned next to her left breast.

"He's *sooo* taken, Jen. Forget it, I don't have a chance."

"Whaddaya talking about?" Jen screams, glaring at the fire. "Get over there, you chickenshit!"

"Forget it Jen! He likes Kat." I grab the bottle from her and take a gulp. "I gotta keep my eye on you anyway, you lush."

Jen mumbles something I don't hear, then slouches down a little lower on the log and hiccups.

"So, ladies, what say we smoke this?" Clive says, exposing his white but crooked teeth. Clive looks so pretty, even with those teeth. Jen calls him a stoner but he's beautiful, he looks like a child: little nose and big lips. And something about the way he looks right at me when he talks sends a wave of nausea to my stomach.

"I don't smoke," I say, looking at Jen.

"Right, don't want to damage those perfect pink runner's lungs, eh, Holly?" he snaps, sticking the joint in his mouth and tapping John for a light.

"How do you know I run?"

"Oh, I take a special interest in young athletes."

It seems rude or something not to accept the joint, so I take a little puff and then cough for about five minutes.

After we smoke, I send Clive and John to ask around for some water for Jen, who is beginning to look a little green, but she gives us a confident thumbs-up whenever we ask how she's doing.

John and Clive come back with a Tupperware container of warm orange juice. Jen takes a big sip and spits it out.

"There's vodka in that!" Jen laughs. John snatches it, sniffs, and takes a gulp.

"I'm getting water," I say. "You jerks stay here and watch her."

As I walk through groups of people sitting on blankets, I pass a black, square-jawed dog, and meet its eyes. I feel flushed from my chest to my crotch, as if there is a candle burning inside me. At peace with the dog, and beers, and fires, I smile at a large girl with long dark hair who's trying to clean the dirt from between her toes. I feel like we're young and, because of this, everything might be OK, if only I could find some water for Jen.

"Hey, Holly!" I turn, clutching the plastic bottle, as Clive trips awkwardly through groups of people: raver girls with sparkles on their faces and platform shoes on their feet, boys with baggy pants, hippies, and people from the dance dressed in various levels of formal attire. Everyone, except Clive, looks shiny. I notice how all his clothes, and his hair, are frayed at the ends and dusty. When he finally gets to me he holds out his hands.

"Thought you might like some company. You going into the school?"

"I guess."

"This way."

He leads me through the crowd, past the car, which is now blaring hip hop, and up a steep dark path. People are arguing about what kind of music to put on next.

"Your school or mine?" He points through the high chain-link fence that separates St. Sebastian from East Tech.

"You go to East Tech?"

"Yessir." He kicks at the fence. East Tech is the last-resort school that specializes in woodworking, mechanics, and "vocational" training—whatever the hell that is. It's the troublemakers' school. You always hear about cars being torched and boys stabbing each other in the halls. There's a reason for the ten-foot spiked fence between East Tech and St. Sebastian. The teachers, especially Mr. Ford, tell us the kids are rowdy, non-Catholic drug addicts. I knew Clive went to a public school, but not East Tech.

"School's not my thing." *No kidding,* I think as he shakes the fence and begins to climb it. I hesitate for a second and then start climbing after him. He sits at the top waiting for me, jiggling around a little, his jeans pulled tight against his bum. We walk along the other side of the fence in the forest for a while in silence.

"You think the school's open?" I ask as we approach a set of orange doors, but really all I can think about is how a guy as nice and calm as Clive managed to get himself into East Tech.

"Wait here," he says, before pulling out a small blade to jimmy the door open. He grabs the juice container from my hands and disappears into the school.

At the top of the hill, after scaling the fence again, we pause to smoke another of Clive's skinny joints.

"So, how'd you get to East Tech?" I ask him.

He looks at me in the growing darkness before plucking the joint from his mouth and passing it to me. His eyes are soft but untrusting. I take a long haul of the pinner, which has some trouble making its way down my throat and into my stomach.

"I yelled at a teacher in my old school. Well, I kind of more than yelled at her."

"What did you do?"

"This woman, this bitch, in grade nine, made me read *The Raisin in a Sun*."

"*A Raisin in* the *Sun*."

"Yeah, whatever, anyway, she was really getting on my nerves, like pushing me . . . I just didn't feel like reading that day."

"So?"

"So, I don't know, I kind of flipped."

"Oh." I hand the joint back to him and look down at the hill. We'll probably have to slide down on our asses to reach the bottom. It's really dark now. I can make out Clive's small nose and his fat lips by the heater of the joint. I contemplate his prettiness, while trying to think of something cool to say.

"We have something in common then."

"What's that?"

"We both got kicked out of school."

"Yeah, John told me about that. Quite the little scrap you ladies got yourselves into." He grins, his teeth glowing.

"Yeah," I sigh, pretending I'm cool and refusing the last of the joint. "So, I figure we slide, ass first, down this hill."

"Just a second." He crushes the roach with his boot and grabs my wrist. Hard.

"You're so pretty, Holly."

I laugh.

He goes for my mouth but I turn my face and he ends up missing it and slobbering down the right side of my cheek. Then he puts his hand under my chin and guides my face to his, and, even in the darkness, I see his eyes close as his face comes closer.

At first I'm nervous, our mouths are so dry from the pot, I can't even move my lips, or find the right way to kiss. But then he finds me, he finds the warm wet place inside my clumsy mouth and pulls my body to his and I am up against his stomach, my hands beneath the back of his shirt. I can't decide what to do next so I try to think of one of the old movies Sol took us to see, *Casablanca*. The image of a suave Humphrey Bogart pressing up against Lauren Bacall. But as I relax into Clive's mouth, I remember that it's only us, two flunkies, tumbling down the hill.

When we get to the bottom I jump ahead of Clive. My arms and legs are scratched up and there's grass in my hair and Clive's laughing so hard he can't get up, so I run on ahead. Jen's safe, thank God, and she seems almost sober now. She still has the baseball hat plastered on her head to hide her hair. I laugh when I see it. Someone has wrapped her in a blanket and she's burping through sips of a huge Coke slurpie and singing along to "Hotel California" with a group of hippies by the dying fire.

Jen offers me a sip of her slurpie as she belches long and happily. I gulp down the Coke and instantly get a head-freeze.

"Ow, ow, ow." I lean my head against her fuzzy blanket, trying to recover.

"Where'd you two disappear to?"

"Just around. We got your water."

"Thanks." She arches her eyebrow. I look around the crowd

and see Clive is on the other side of the fire. He's got his shirt off and is hackey-sacking with a group of kids. Jen follows my gaze and then pokes me in the ribs.

"Hey, stop drooling."

"Shut up."

"Looks like . . ."

"What!?"

"I was going to *say,* before I was so rudely interrupted, that it looks like you found someone as freaky as you."

# chapter 30

There were lights inside me in surgery. I joked with the anesthesiologist before I went under.

"Are you a heart surgeon?" I asked stupidly, drunk with my first heady, airless breath of the stuff. I'm one of those annoying chatty and aggressive patients; I figure there's no other way to be under the knife.

"No, dear," the surgeon said as the nurse adjusted his glasses. "I'm a gynecologist."

The black hole of anesthesia, the smell of hospitals barely masking vomit and blood; it all colludes in re-creating the memory that runs like a surreal colourized movie over and over in my head. And now I'm certain that it happened:

I'm dressed, so nicely, in a flowered pink dress, white ballet leotards, and shiny, black patent-leather shoes. Holly's with a babysitter for my "appointment" today, so I have our parents all to myself. It's a rare day of indulgence for me: a trip to the toy store and the book store. One toy and all the books I want and then a Disney movie. All efforts to forget, to erase the smell of burnt hair and the shiny patches of gel on my back and temples.

My head's buzzing, filled with the sound of a *rat-a-tat-tat*, like a birthday-cake sparkler fizzing out. I *pop, pop, pop* so I hop, hop, hop, hop on *pop*—over puddles, my mother is holding my hand, leading me along the busy downtown streets after a quick spring rain.

Dad buys me a strawberry cone from a street stall to match my dress. He bends down on one knee to offer it to me.

"There you go, sweetheart." He pats my head. Vesla yanks me away, nearly causing me to drop my hard-won treat. I scowl at her, smile up at his head, which has a hat on it. Hats are funny, I think in my child-head. *Hats are like socks for your head.* I study my perfect little black shoe as the cold sweet cream trickles down my throat.

"Are you satisfied?" She glares at Thomas, pinning her free arm to her side, refusing the plain vanilla cone he offers her. He leans his head to one side, as if he thinks her question is absurd; the edge of his hat threatens to tip over like a sinking boat. Then he nods and, walking away from us, begins to eat the melting ice cream himself.

"Hats are funny!" I scream. He stops to look back, his eyebrows arched high, before my knees turn to rubber and I sway down.

During an epileptic seizure, the EEG records brain waves—interictal brain waves—which may or may not show evidence of seizure activity. Safe and painless, the procedure requires that electrodes be attached to the skull to record brain currents; however, they do not deliver electricity to the scalp.

"Bring my medical encyclopedia tomorrow."
  "What letter?"
  "E."

Sphenoidal electrodes record electrical activity in the front deep sections of the temporal and frontal lobes. For this procedure, a needle is inserted into the cheek and a wire is inserted into the skin.

Mom sits with me most afternoons, reading me magazines, filling me in on gossip at the hospital, and wiping my face with a cold washcloth. I smile at her and try to look interested. I take the photo of Misha out of my journal and put it in her magazine. She doesn't look up. Instead, she looks at the photo, studying his image. There is a vague resemblance between Misha and Thomas; both have large jawlines, dark hair, and high cheekbones, only Thomas's eyes are a startling blue and Misha's are brown.

  "Tell me the end of the story."
  "I've told you already."
  "I forget, tell me again."

A good physician places the safety and the best interests of the individual patient above all else.

Misha has Thomas cornered in the tiny wooden shed lined with garden tools. In the middle of the shed there is a small card table with several chairs around it. Thomas is seated in one of the corner chairs, and Misha, the taller and stronger of the two men, is wrapping coarse rope around Thomas's wrists, binding them together. Thomas kicks against the chair, pleading, "Misha, I know you don't like me."

"Yes, you know that at least. I hate you. I hate the way you talk, the way you walk, the way you look at my wife."

"She's not your wife, not yet."

Misha pulls the rope so it cuts Thomas.

"You must tell her, you must tell someone, Misha, for the love of God, you've got epilepsy, there's medication. You can't hide it, it's dangerous."

Misha cinches the knot; Thomas feels the burning in his wrists cutting right down to his bone.

Misha overturns the small card table, then he aims, and kicks Thomas square in the stomach. Thomas doubles over, feeling a trace of spittle trickle down his cheek.

"You're to stay away from me, from Vesla, from my friends. I'll have a servant untie you and then you will take the next train back to the city. If I see or hear from you ever again I'll have you killed." Misha crouches over Thomas; their faces are close enough for Thomas to smell the alcohol and dill on Misha's breath.

"But we can do something, we can treat you. The others don't have to know."

"I am sick of sharing secrets with you."

Misha rises and turns as Thomas wriggles out of the rope and leaps over the upturned table, but Misha has already slipped out the door. Thomas stabs his hand into the space where the door is cracked open, between the small crevice where the light, the forest, the world, leaks in. But Misha slams the door violently, crushing the top knuckles of Thomas's fingers. Thomas, in too much pain to start screaming yet, hears the snap of a lock on the outside.

Later, when they've pulled Misha's body to shore, and the ambulance has come and gone, a maid arrives to unlock Thomas from the shed and she screams when she sees him, sitting by the wall, cradling his broken fingers.

When he's let out, he doesn't go to comfort her, instead he runs up the hill, behind the house, towards the train tracks. He crouches like a sniper, in a ditch, head throbbing, fingers numb. He runs again, his heartbeats double, then triple. He stops at the top and rests, looking over at the illuminated house from which her wailing rises. He takes his pulse and thinks of the unborn child, before rising and walking along the train tracks. And then there is nothing in his mind but the bright hot fear of death.

The fact that a patient is going to die does not necessarily mean he should be operated on.

"He thought that it would ruin his career if the others knew. He thought Thomas was there to tell them—about me, about the epilepsy, everything. Expose him. That's why he locked him in that stupid shed," she says, rolling my fingers in her palm so hard it hurts.

"Maybe he thought Thomas would try to save him, Ma, maybe that's why he locked him in. Maybe he didn't drown by accident, maybe . . ."

Mom pulls away from me and looks at my forehead, dragging her hands through my dry, stiff plaits of hair.

"I tried resuscitation, I breathed into him for twenty minutes. I tried everything. I'm a nurse. I—"

"I know, Ma, I know."

"Misha's career was the most important thing to him, and weakness, of any kind, was not tolerated among party members."

"Is that why?"

"Is that why, what?"

"Is that why you fell for Thomas?"

Mom cradles her head in her hands.

"Just tell me, tell me about it. I want to know, Ma. I just need to know. It doesn't matter if you cheated on Misha, now."

"I don't know how. One day we bumped into each other, at a park. We started talking . . . went out for dinner—Misha was out of town—we caught up, gossiped about our little town. Your father seemed so free, you know how Holly has that quality, like she doesn't care, about rules, what's next, about what she's supposed to do."

"Yeah."

"That's what Thomas was like. He couldn't schmooze, he couldn't pretend to accept all that *communista* stuff, he just couldn't."

"And you liked that about him."

Mom sees me shiver and pulls the sheet up over my knees.

"Yes, I loved that about him," she says almost defiantly.

"Because you didn't accept it either."

"That, and Misha had so many secrets, so many pressures . . ."

"And Dad didn't have any?"

"None, not like Misha anyway. No secrets, except for me."

There's a long pause and, somehow, I find the strength to lean over and hug Mom. We hold each other that way for a while, not talking or moving, as if nothing came before this moment and nothing will come after it.

"Do you blame me, Gizella?" she asks over my shoulder, quietly.

"I can never know what it was like for you, so I can't, I can't judge you. I just need to know that you married my father."

"I did." Mom holds my head in her hands and examines my eyes. Then I get the image of the river in my head, pulling Misha down, away, like a torn branch wrenched from a trunk, and suddenly, it hits me: she has no idea.

# chapter 31

Giselle had to have an emergency operation called a laparoscopy. She has endometriosis, and what happens is the lining of her uterus was growing all over the place where it shouldn't have been—in her stomach, on her ovaries. That's what was causing her so much pain with her period.

After the operation, they wheeled Giselle back to her room and I sat next to her, watching her breathe. Watching her made me sleepy so I slept too, for a while. I woke up because I heard someone in the room. It was the doctor, a young guy, who was not much older than Giselle. He looked at her chart, although the only light in the room was from the hallway fluorescent. I wanted him to go away; surely there was someone having a heart attack somewhere who needed him. I crossed my arms over my chest and stood yawning over Giselle, who was still dead asleep.

"The stitches are tiny. A couple here—" he pointed to his belly button, poking himself like the Pillsbury doughboy "—and three on her lower stomach. Her skin's still young. You'll barely be able to see a scar." He smiled.

I nodded and toyed with one of Giselle's IV tubes, untwisting it, thinking about the small, careful cross-stitching on her stomach that would one day allow her to wear a bikini, shamelessly. I didn't have the heart to tell the doctor that my sister goes to the beach fully clothed. But I knew if Giselle was awake she'd appreciate his handiwork, his skilful pale hands, and the cream he would suggest she rub on it to speed healing.

"Good night," he said. "If she wakes up and needs anything, just call one of the nurses."

I smiled at him and he left the half-lit room for the too-bright hallway. Giselle's breathing seemed laboured. I closed the door, turned on the small bedside light, and lifted her gown to examine the angry little pink scar the doctor seemed so proud of. Hopeful is not what I should have felt then, looking at Giselle's ribs, her hipbones sticking out. Hopeful, her breathing wasn't. Her weight, even with the clear white syrup food feeding her shell, was anything but hopeful, and yet something about that tiny, almost seamless line spoke to me of hope. I memorized its hooked route on her skin as I watched my sister shift in her sleep.

Maybe she was moving in a dream where summer, her favourite season, wasn't passing her by, where she had the chance to streak into the water, her white skin flashing above the tiny waves between patches of lights, her body bending beneath the tow in one easy triple motion: her arms kissing the sky, the rocks, and then lifting her to surface, afloat.

. . .

Agnes and I are waiting in the coffee shop that faces the mental hospital. Mom's late. We're taking Agnes to see Giselle today. Galaxy Donuts has a steady stream of homeless and crazy people who walk in and out demanding weird things they don't sell at a doughnut shop, like roast beef sandwiches, while the Korean girl at the counter screams, "Watt?! Cream?"

A little girl is sitting on the floor next to our stools. Occasionally she gets up to wrap her legs around the metal pole of my stool. Agnes mumbles about the poison in the doughnuts as purple jelly spurts across her cheek.

I tell Agnes about Giselle, about the operation. I tell her I'm going to be hanging out with her some days, when Mom has a lot of patients to see. I also tell Agnes that if she thinks she's going to try that cigarette-swallowing trick, the one she tried with Giselle, she's even crazier than anybody knows, because I know the Heimlich maneuver. I karate-chop the counter to show Agnes my violent tendencies, that she shouldn't even *think* of messing with me. She bugs her eyes out and makes an expression I might mistake as rage mixed with respect. As Agnes gulps down the last bit of dough and tries to wipe the white powder off her face, the little girl untangles herself from my stool and starts pulling on my pants.

"Miss," she says, all polite-like.

"What?"

"Look." She points out the window at the huge, sprawling, grey mental hospital across the street. "That's where the crazy people live."

I nod, hoping Agnes hasn't heard, but she's too absorbed in trying to light her cigarette.

"Do you know someone who lives there?" she asks me, watching Agnes's ashes float to the floor.

. . .

Instead of going to the hospital with Mom and Agnes, I go to the court to shoot hoops with Clive. It has become a ritual with us: I shoot while he smokes up. We don't talk much; with school over, the only thing I have to talk about these days is Giselle. And this makes me sad and makes Clive sad, so we try to talk about other stuff.

Later we'll go into the long grass behind the school where the yellow leaves have started to smell bonfire smoky, and paw at each other's summer sweaters. Kissing so warm you feel like you are in the person's mouth.

Clive grabs the rebound off the board and tries a jumpshot. He dribbles out and offers me a drag of his joint.

"Just a small one."

"I had an idea."

"Oh yeah."

I know all about his ideas. Like hitchhiking up to my cottage sometime soon, like playing drums all day, naked, eating nothing but melon and talking about Gandhi. Like fixing an old motorcycle and training me for a marathon.

He tries a layup, which he misses, and then elaborates on his idea, bouncing the ball towards me.

"We'll smoke pot with your sister."

I net the ball from the three-quarter point.

"Bingo, your getting that ball in the net was a check mark, like a shooting star." The confidence of the stoned individual is truly amazing.

"That was no shooting star, you goon. We are *not* smoking with her."

"I think it would be great ... She could relax, get the munchies, it's supposed to be really good for what she's got."

"I think it's a great idea, Clive, but we'll wait until she gets off the intravenous first. Okay?"

He doesn't say anything, just closes his eyes, acting all stoned.

I miss the shot and look at him. I stick my tongue out. He runs up and pitches his body at me, then places his forehead on my neck, his hair falling down my shirt.

I think about how, since I've met Clive, I haven't cut or fallen or bruised myself once. I hold him up as the light summer wind wraps his hair around my face, as if Clive was the girl and I was the boy.

. . .

I wait until I see Sol get his coffee in the cafeteria. I hide behind the steel doors. His hair is long and greasy, his beard is growing in. I follow him to his car, watch him put three creams in his coffee, set it in the cup holder, and rev his engine. He's taken to sitting by her bedside for hours, waiting, watching, holding her hand. He goes to her in the morning, before work, arrives at about five and sits there till ten to nine. He talks to her like she's in a coma and I guess she sort of is because she sleeps mostly. I don't know what he says: probably that he loves her, that he needs her back, who knows. I don't know where this sleep comes from either; they're probably giving her drugs. Maybe she's just tired. The doctor said everyone reacts differently to surgery, that the body repairs itself in sleep. He also said that since Giselle's so skinny, and she lost so much blood, she needs extra recovery time and care because she's seriously weak and anemic.

When Sol leaves, I run up the stairs, two at a time, into her hospital room. I stare at her bones. You can make out the shape of her skull around her eyes. Giselle's lost almost thirty pounds since last month. Last week she hit a new low: eighty-seven pounds.

I walk around her bed, sniff at the bouquets Sol has brought her, prop up the card with the message "GET WELL SOON!" in gold block letters, superimposed on the heads of fluffy white kittens, signed "Agnes." Jesus, Giselle, you know you're in trouble when Agnes is giving you get well cards. I sift through the boxes of chocolates people have sent her, sucking on the caramel ones and pitching the coconut ones in the trash. Giselle hates coconut. People are so stupid, you wouldn't believe it, sending anorexics boxes of Laura Secord. I putter around the room making sure everything's in order, then I sit on the little green plastic chair next to her bed and shake her.

"What?" She rubs her eyes.

"You look like hell."

"Thanks."

"You do."

"What's new?" She sniffs at the air and then gags, sticking her tongue out in a way that always makes me laugh.

"Listen to me, they scraped around in your gut."

She tries to sit up and winces. Then she puts her hands on her stomach. "Don't touch it!" I whip her hand off the stitches and attract the attention of a nurse walking down the hall. She pokes her head in the room.

"Everything OK in here?"

"Great, thanks." I grin, then face Giselle again. "I'm telling you, this is serious."

"No more spicy food?"

"That's the least of your worries. Look, the doctor says you lost a lot of blood. You have to be careful. You have to eat, Giselle, build up some reserves."

"So, I'm not dying?" Giselle smiles.

"How did you get so goddamn morbid?"

"I dunno. Ask Thomas."

She looks away for a minute, clears her throat, then asks for her diary.

"It's in the drawer." I make a move to pull it open for her, but then I let her struggle for a minute. She's too weak to sit herself up and twist around to get it. Something sick in me doesn't help her. Finally something breaks in me, my sister

207

breaks in me, my fucking sister, looking so small, like the half-dead AIDS patients shuffling around downstairs, smoking cigarettes. This, ladies and gentlemen, this is my sister. I hand the diary to her.

"You brought my books, too?" She's all lit up because we brought her doctor books: pages and pages of diagrams, charts, information Giselle devours over and over. She's jealous, she probably wishes she could've operated on herself.

She opens up her diary to a clean page in the middle, then asks for a pen. I go out into the hall and beg the nurse for the pink pen on a string around her neck and bring it back to Giselle. She writes furiously for a while and then pauses.

"The doctor said you can still have kids."

She looks at me sharply. "Bullshit. He didn't say that."

"OK, you're right, he didn't."

She looks out the window, and the way the muted light from the clouds hits her makes me want to take a picture of her. Even though her face has sunken in, Giselle still looks beautiful. No wonder Sol sits here for four hours, counting the shades of green in her face.

"I have a boyfriend," I say suddenly, not knowing exactly why. Giselle cranks out a toothy smile and closes her book.

"Tell me, tell me all about him."

. . .

When I get back from lunch, Giselle's sleeping and Sol's standing at the window of her room talking to the pigeons on the ledge. I pull on his untucked shirt ends. He reels back and catches my elbow to steady himself.

"Hey, you scared the shit outta me," he whispers, his eyes bloodshot and leaking. He looks like he's wearing white powder makeup and his lips are a windblown ruby colour. It looks like someone clocked him in the face but obviously he hasn't been sleeping.

"What's today been like?" I ask, hovering over Giselle. He shrugs and looks back at the pigeon outside.

"I don't know." He paces the room.

"How're tricks, Sol? Besides this."

"Tricks are shit, Holly. I got schlepping coffees, copies . . . grunt work, a couple of leads, and this, I have this."

When he's not here, he's at work, or in his car, or at his dad's, doing Sol things: smoking, drinking, writing stories and stuff for the paper, thinking about Giselle, worrying.

"How is it for you?" he says quietly, his red eyes on Giselle, who tries to turn in her bed.

"OK, I guess."

He steps back from the bed, grabs my hand, then pulls me to him and hugs me from behind. Hard. I smell the stale smell of nicotine, sweat, and that sandalwood again.

He begins talking in my ear. "I remember the first time I saw you play basketball. Giselle dragged me to one of your games, your arm was hurt."

"Sprained. I sprained it playing volleyball."

"Yeah, you'd just got your hair cut. It stood straight up, super short. You kept wiping your nose and screaming for the ball the whole game. You shot well."

"Forty."

"Forty, yeah. The whole time she's sitting next to me yelling her brains out. I swear to God my arm was bruised she hit me so many times saying, 'That's my sister, isn't she amazing?' You looked so cute in your green shorts, Holly, and that plastic yellow basketball mesh. I didn't know who I loved more then, you or her." He laughs.

"Sol, you're a perv." I push him away.

I peer into his black eyes and see the reflection of who she

209

once was. I see their couldhavebeentomorrows flicker silver, the ghost of her spirit throwing light all over the drab hospital room.

I see fields, open and wide with white flowers, the countries they would travel to, the wines they would drink, grenadine spilling from their mouths, Sol blowing smoke into her mouth and saying:

"Oh, G.! You're the most beautiful woman in the whole-world baby you are all my best parts. I could crash like a gasoline fire into your arms every night and no one could care but you and that would be a-okay with me honey, as long as we burn together and not out tonight."

And in the blackness round his eyes I see the hard times, too, her hands flying up to strike his head, blood leaking from it, her medication, his boozing, tantrums, fights, her, like this. I see them together, dressed as bride and groom, gritting their teeth with laughter, moving forward in slow-motion time, while some great big brass marching band plays out of tune.

"Coming?" he says, offering his hand, breaking up the silent parade.

Giselle is tapping her finger on her sheet, as if she hears all this. Though it is only midmorning, Sol's spent. His body goes limp as he trudges to the heavy green door.

"Come on, I'll give you a ride home if you want. I just have to stop in at the office first, pick up some stuff for a story." His jaw clenches and unclenches as he runs his hand over Giselle's paper forehead. "And, after, we could get some ice cream, drop back in and bring G. some. We'll get her favourite, strawberry."

I squeeze her hand and kiss it.

"Stay with me today, Holly, I don't feel like being alone, what do you say?" He smiles slowly as if it hurts his face.

I pick a curl from the back of his head and stroke it. He turns and gives me a dead stare. I take my hand back.

"Sol, you need to sleep, you look . . . you look awful."

He says nothing, but pulls on a new, expensive pair of sun-glasses that make him look like a fly-eyed rock star. I follow him out, guiltily, leaving the wedding march behind, leaving Giselle entirely to her thick sleep. Fearful of all the noise he and I make, so close to her.

# chapter 32

Typically, a vertical skin incision is required to perform thorough abdominal exploration because purulent fluid may be located between loops of bowel for endometriosis, symptoms of which are: pelvic pain, dysmenorrhea, infertility, menstrual problems, and dyspareunia.

Dear sweet Jesus. I only wanted a body like my sister's, strong and lean and winsome. Impervious to weather, impervious to bending and bleeding. Okay, that's not true, Holly bleeds. I've seen the thick matted wads in the wastebasket; while I buried mine in the bottom of the garbage can so no one would know I had my period, Holly didn't seem to care who saw what.

Holly always revels in the early days of it, slugging back a carton of chocolate milk and moaning on the couch until she goes for an hour-long run, swearing it's the only thing that makes the cramps go away.

Me? I popped caffeine pills and fed on carrot sticks, devising ways of eliminating the problem altogether. Now all those bloodless months seem to have caught up with me.

When I ask Holly where the clothes I wore to the hospital are, she makes a face and says, "I don't think you want those, G."

"Why?"

"We kinda had to throw them out."

"Why?"

Holly's face looks concentrated. She goes to the bedside table and pops open the small makeup mirror I'd asked Mom to bring me so I could pluck my eyebrows. I haven't yet checked my appearance. Holly looks away when she hands it to me. And there, staring back, is the lioness, with the same defiant look in her eye, the same heavy jaw, only less ferocious somehow. Airless, bloodless, her head shorn of light.

Surgery exposes patients to four main risks: 1) the theatre air; 2) surgical instruments and materials used in operation; 3) the surgical staff in the operating theatre; and 4) the patient herself.

At night, the buzzing sound of the hospital keeps me awake. I can hear the gurgle of the boiler, the quiet laughter of nurses at the desk, the coffee machine plunking cups down, not to mention all the wheezing machinery keeping us corpses alive.

At night the springs of the bed twist into my spine and cut into me. No matter which way I turn, it feels as if there is a cigar being constantly extinguished in the centre of my back. But I'm embarrassed about asking for more meds.

At night the aching in my gut and bones is unbearable. I stare out the window, at the street lamps, hoping that they'll distract me. The ache starts out hot, deep in the crevice of my centre, and expands out, wrapping itself around my intestines, and then burns up out of my skin. It appears as sweat on the surface though, tiny tearlike beads, a cold-sweat fever. Usually I swing my leg out from under the eight blankets piled up on me and search with my toe for the cold tile floor. But I never reach it.

Two days ago I tried and fell off the bed. I must have done a flip in the air or something because now I'm covered with bruises. I lay there for about forty minutes before calling out to a nurse. I tried to get up by myself but the floor seemed just as comfortable as the bed, so I stayed there shivering, applauding the hospital ventilation system for the arctic temperatures it's able to maintain.

A nurse shuffled into my room and found me. She picked me up like a baby, covered me in blankets and then she did a strange thing: she kissed me on the forehead and stroked my head, saying my name over and over until even the burning pain faded and I couldn't feel the bruises.

I used to be able to do one-handed cartwheels. On our dry summer lawn, with a Popsicle in my mouth . . . Holly finally taught me how. I used to torment my sister by pinning her down and licking her face as she whipped her hair at me. I used to take aqua-fitness classes with old ladies, just for kicks. After staying up all night studying for a biology exam, I once split a twenty-six of Jack Daniel's with Susan and we showed up to an awful, boring-ass med party screaming, "Screw yew!" in a Scottish accent, at the top of our lungs. There was a time when I had so many things to do that I couldn't remember them all and had to write them down on scraps of paper. I used to go out for dinners with Sol and we'd hold hands and gaze at one another—The Way That Young Lovers Do. Our voices were earnest and soft as we spilled wine on the white tablecloth and traded secrets.

These are now the memories of an altogether different person. I've traded my breath for phlegm. For cold-sweat fever. The taste of steel and honey in my mouth defeats me.

Endometriosis is one of the main causes of infertility: 30 to 40 percent of women with endometriosis are barren.

Scrape scrape goes the knife. Scrape scrape goes my life. I am a human abortion. I am nothing.

I had to send Sol away today. In his reflection I could see my looks fading, the gripping sorrow in his eyes for its passing, saying quietly, when he thought I couldn't hear him, saying, "Please girl, please get yourself together."

Vanity, a terrible beast, exists even in the most hideous of humans, this shell of a woman shrinking in her ex-lover's eyes. He brought me oatmeal cookies. He ate one and I ate two. The doctor will be happy. This means I can go for a walk down the hall. Holly will take me.

There were days when I ran on nothing but a small crouching pain in my gut that ate me up from the inside out, and now it's finally won. I guess I'm paying for all those missed dinners and periods, for all my thoughts of immortality. I'm a med student, I know the rules of the body, energywise: put nothing in and nothing comes out. So, why, after so long of putting nothing inside I have all this stuff pouring out? Where does it come from?

When Holly comes to visit, I ask her to bring my black jeans, some T-shirts, and a sweater. She looks at me curiously.

"Come on, I can only wear this fleecy robe for so long, I have to start getting dressed." Holly comes over and stands close to my bed.

"OK, but you have to eat this." She hands me an apple and three more cookies. I look at her despairingly. Feeling sorry for me, she pulls out her Swiss Army knife and cuts up the apple and we share it; she gives me really thin slices. There's a strict caloric rule if I want to get off the tubes: at least three thousand calories a day. I cut a deal with the doctor.

I pull my bank card out of my diary and hand it to Holly. "Take out a hundred dollars and bring it by tonight."

"Giselle—"

"Just do it!"

She looks at the card. "If you run away, you have to let me find you."

"I'm not going anywhere. Look at me! I just want to order some pizzas for the floor." I grin.

"You hate pizza."

She puts the card in her jeans and proceeds to crumble the cookie into her hand, feeding me chocolate chips with her long, thin fingers.

A curette is used to scrape out the uterus.

Tonight a new dream: when I fall away, I fall into space, without electrodes pulling me down. Female hands stroke my body, they move up and down, with gentle insistence, over my arms, legs, face. I know whose fingers they are, not Holly's, not Eve's. They fold into me like wings, flutter against my side. They pull me up until suddenly I'm sitting up in bed.

Awake, finally, for the first time in days, I feel somewhat normal, or at least less foggy in the head and less achy. I pull out the catheter and step off the bed. It feels like walking on the moon, only I'm steady, I don't fall this time: my bare foot hits the cold tiled floor and I find the pants Holly brought, laid across the chair. I pull them on, cinch the belt tight so they stay on.

—*There you go.*

I pull out five twenties and my card.

"Thank you," I whisper, pulling on my T-shirt, not worrying about a bra because my breasts are so small. On the chair is Agnes's purse, the golden chintzy one she gave to Holly recently. I open it and inside are Dad's monkey skull, a handful of chocolate bars, and a tube of Agnes's crazy orange lipstick. I walk into the washroom, flick the light on but then catch a glimpse of something so hideous my hand slaps at the wall.

—*Good girl. Don't need to see that right now.*

—Oh my God. Oh my Jesus Christ. Have you seen what we look like?

—*I have.*

I try to block out the image of the bony girl with green teeth who is supposed to be me. I grab the purse and focus on finding some shoes. My search leads me to a pair of Hawaiian-print flip-flops that will have to do. I flip-flop around the bed with them, trying to see if I can flip quietly; I manage a shuffling sound that may be mistaken by a nurse for an old man journeying to the toilet. I'm so excited in my new clothes; I keep running my hands over my body, feeling its sharp edges.

—*The important thing now is not to think about your appearance. The important thing now is to focus on the task at hand: getting out of here.*

—But where are we going?

—*It doesn't matter. I don't know about you, but I've just about had it with hospitals. Let's finish this somewhere private.*

—OK, I wouldn't mind a hamburger, actually.

—*A hamburger?!*

I start trembling. We've come so far, now this. I sink to the floor, placing my palms face down. Now I've gone and made her roar. Stupid, stupid, stupid. Now she'll never let me go.

Feral and starved, all I can think of, though, is getting that blood back somehow, getting some meat. I rub my collarbone; she sniffs with indifference but acquiesces, slowly evening out her breathing. A lion, after all, likes her pound of flesh.

—Did I say hamburger? I meant cheeseburger.

# chapter 33

Dear God, it's me Margaret (just kidding, it's Holly),

I never ask for anything. I know I got kicked out of school. Sorry.

(And if you are reading this, if he is reading this, Hi Dad! Hi!) You did take him away and it's not a count against you or anything like that, I'm just saying, it's been pretty rotten for me, Mom, and Giselle since he left.

But you know all about THAT and this isn't about him, it's about Giselle. If you could help her in some way I'd be really grateful and go to church or pray or read to blind people or do whatever you want me to do (just let me know).

See, all I want is for my sister, Giselle Vasco, to get better and be a doctor or do whatever it is she wants.

Since you can read my mind anyway, I won't even pretend to make this a selfless act because it isn't. I just feel like no one in this house can live their lives until she gets better and that it's taking my life, shabby and unformed as it is, away.

Also today my mother was on her way to work and

tripped and fell on something in front of the house and she couldn't get up and just kept crying and crying until I had to bring her inside and put her to bed and she couldn't go to work because her ankle was twisted and because she thinks Giselle is going to die.

Plus, yesterday Giselle's hair fell out. Her long ropy blond dreads just sort of detached themselves from her head and it was really sad to see and I tried to pull them all off the pillow and hide her hair while she was sleeping but she woke up anyway, half-bald, and started screaming, "Am I in f—ing chemo!?" (sorry again) and then she started crying and crying, too, just like Mom, over her hair, even though, as you know, lately she's had a lot more to cry about.

So if you could stop all the crying and let me know where I could put my sister's hair and/or make her better I'd REALLY appreciate it.

Thank you for your time<br>Holly Vasco

P.S. I have always loved you.

. . .

I sit in the car with the radio turned up high while Sol double-parks and runs into the newsroom.

Giselle once told me that if Sol had the ambition he could easily end up being a section editor in a couple of years, if he wanted, but that he doesn't really care.

"He's got a fear of success," Giselle told me, sucking on a lollipop in front of the television. "Which goes with a fear of failure, you know, so he'll just stay in the same place forever. But at least he can do something, besides drink." Giselle had this sort of untouchable look when she snorted that out, like she thought she was better than Sol. Her expression made me want to smack her in the face, to really hurt her. It made me want to ask her where exactly she thought she was a-moving-and-a-shakin-to, watching "Laverne and Shirley" reruns, wearing fuzzy zebra slippers, and eating Tootsie Rolls in her ratty underwear.

I snoop through Sol's glove compartment while he goes into the building. It's the usual stuff: registration, bolts, beer caps, a stale cigarette, and a Polaroid shot of Giselle dancing at a club, with her eyes half-closed, singing into a beer bottle. She's wearing a bright orange tank top, her dreads are pulled into a loose but neat ponytail, and she looks happy. I wonder who took the picture and try to think of the last time she went dancing and can't remember.

Then I see him through the glass, looking out the window across the clutter of news desks and monitors. The newsroom is on street level, its windows are transparent, and the office space is open concept so you can watch all the busy media people working from the street. Posed against this backdrop of people and activity, he seems strong, capable of making split-second decisions—crack a joke, or pull a knife? His body is lean and solid, I've seen it bounce off his night-blue chrome car, seen him crash affectionately against Giselle in a mock-tackle.

You should see your boy-man, G. He's just like you, toxic, addicted to the speed of his own destruction. What could you possibly give him when there is so little of you left? While you sleep off the pounds he drowns his perpetual hangovers with pills and, some days, he coughs blood.

Inside the building, I can see punchy, punky little women moving around handing out memos, people talking on the phone. I imagine the din of typing, the office gossip, the sound of laughter, computer beeps, ringing phones. But Sol doesn't seem to hear or see any of these things. Amid all the million little hurt and strained egos, the hacked-off human remains, bar brawls and car accidents and office politics, he looks at me in the car, mouths the word "deadline," as if, for the first time in his life, he knows what it means.

. . .

Energized by a good cry, three shots of whisky, and half a litre of orange-chocolate ice cream, we drive back to the hospital. Sol's got a paper bag full of treats for Giselle: ice cream, stick-on tattoos, hair clips. Buying her things makes him feel good, though I wonder what he thinks she'll do with pink barrettes now that she has only white and fuzzy tufts of hair. He whistles a little, and, though the veins near his eyes are bulging out from crying, he seems OK for now.

"Hello," he calls in a falsetto, knocking at her door as he clutches the bag expectantly. "Where are youuuuu . . . ?" The door swings open and reveals Giselle's empty bed. Her white twisted sheets lie in a heap to one side. Her intravenous has leaked all over the edge of the mattress and makes a soft dripping sound as it hits the floor in steady drops.

A chubby little blond nurse sees us standing in the door and walks into the room. She notices the tube and starts to disassemble the contraption.

"Ah, excuse me," I say, while Sol continues to stare at the vacated bed.

"Do you know where my sister is?" I ask the nurse, who is pulling the sheets off the bed. "She's supposed to be here."

"Your sister?" she says, putting her hands on her hips as if she is about to lecture me on sisterhood. "Is gone."

# chapter 34

A good surgical team is happy that the patient is awake, stable, and comfortable.

One step in front of the other, one step. Flip. Flop.

—*That was easy.*

Almost too easy, I think as a cab pulls up in front of the side doors of the hospital to sweep me away like some crusty Cinderella reject. I climb in and request a ride to the east end from the nice man in the turban driving my pumpkin-chariot. He drops me off at a diner I used to go to for greasy fries and milkshakes not far from the mental hospital. Frequented by hustlers and homeless guys, the diner is a good place to hang out; no one gives me a second glance under the fluorescent lights; they figure I'm some junkie seeking a high, which, in some ways, I guess I am.

One step in front of another, I flip-flop my way to an orange booth without dropping my tray. Things are just terrific until the guy behind the counter walks by my table and deposits a warmish ketchup bottle on my table.

"Here you go, sir," he says.

—*Sir?*

I devour the food in front of me, trying to block out the sound of AM radio in my ears, feeling for the wad of cash in my jeans, trying not to think about where I will go next, if I ever dare to leave the diner.

My mouth feels swathed in grease and gauze. I grin into the mirror alongside the booth ... my teeth are smeared with ketchup. Suddenly the image of Thomas's fat, greasy heart leaps into my head. Numbed but throbbing, unable, unable to—

—All I ever did was love him.

"I'd like the heart-attack special," I used to say to the man at the counter, who no longer recognizes me as a girl. I can't get it out of my head now, the arteries globbed with bile, with cigarette smoke, anxiety swarming in liquid poison; my father's overheated core.

—*Flip-flop, my heart is attacked.*


Knowledge of anatomy changes from a way to perform a cadaver's dissection to a practical understanding of why drawing arterial blood from the wrong site can injure your patient.


When I shuffle out of the diner, feeling both excited and shaky, there is a real-live tranny junkie sitting on the corner, selling all her earthly wares, including Tikki cups, on a stained, pink blanket.

"How much for the Expos hat?" I ask, sucking in my cheeks to look even more terrifying. The dyed-blond, who could be either ten years older or younger than me, doesn't seem to notice how freaky I look. Like me, she's sort of a she-male, but she's bulky, and she's trying to feed crackers to a stuffed bear-clown doll she has bundled in a blue, pilled blanket. Without interrupting her cooing, she sticks out her hand and barks: "Two-fifty!"

"Two-fifty? How 'bout an even three?"

I put the money down on the pink blanket and grab the hat. I pull it over my skull and bend the front.

"Lookin' good, Angie!" she chirps, giving me an enthusiastic thumbs-up. I grin back at her, comforted by the sight of someone who looks as rough as me. As I make my way to the corner I hear her call out to me and I turn back. She waves the baby-blue blanket at me. "Angie! Wait!"

"What?"

She walks over, all leg in her three-inch heels, and puts the blanket in my arms.

"I thought it was for your, ah, baby."

She doesn't say anything, instead she presses two hot quarters into my hand.

"Your change."

And, for the first time in weeks, someone looks into my face, not afraid of what they'll see. I look up at her, at the caked mascara creeping off her singed eyelashes, at the deep unforgiving lines in her face, at the foundation that sticks like cracked glue to the five o'clock shadow creeping over her jawline. I feel grateful for this soiled but practical item, for being noticed.

"You're not Angie," she says, studying my forehead. My stomach lets out an agonized groan as she turns on her heel, saying, "Take the blanket. Wherever you're going, honey, it looks like you'll need it."

The recovery room has continuity with the operating room, so that the anesthesiologist and surgeon remain aware of the patient's condition and remain available in the event of complications.

I shuffle through a fishy-smelling alleyway holding the stiff blanket.

I am here. I am alone.

—*Well, almost.*

I am in my black jeans, my white shirt, and my blue cap, carrying Agnes's purse. I am in the world, in this city. I have a right. I am alive now.

I walk alongside Dumpsters, over sewer drains, behind bars and restaurants. I can hear voices, the clang of streetcar bells, men laughing, babies crying. I hear the blood pumping through me, what little remains, I hear it, coursing through me in magnificent waves of pain and then again that desperate, malcontent, pounding heart.

What was it like for him? Going under, awash in his own secretions. Full of the stuff. I walk till I can't anymore, till my feet are filthy with Chinatown smells and the thong in the plastic flip-flop has blistered my toes. I sit down by a fire escape, wrapping the blankie over my shoulders. Waiting for my name to come back to me, I sit on the back step in a dark alley, trying to breathe, thinking I am stuck in the clogs of a dead man's heart and the lapse in another man's brain.

—Who made me, anyway?

—*You are trash, born out of two men.*

—No.

—*It's important to know the origins of "Who," isn't it, Doctor?*

—Yes.

—*Epilepsy is passed through the father's genes. Isn't that right? Isn't that why he had the EEG done?*

If an EEG is performed in a hospital or at a large office practice, more than one neurologist is able to review the results, thus lessening subjectivity and bias.

A week after the tests, the buzzing in my body, along with the memory of the appointment, fades. I can only hold on to flashes of that day: Dad's grey hat bobbing in a crowd of heads, a lump of strawberry ice cream on my shoe. But I can't remember what happened when the black cords were on me and a soft white noise filled my nose like ginger ale. I know only that that day is the reason my parents are still not speaking to each other.

Then one morning the phone rings before school. Daddy picks up and nods, not saying anything, except, "Thank you," at the end of the conversation. I am mashing my eggs into a ketchupy lump, Holly's concentrating on holding a juice cup without dropping it, and our eyes are fixed on the small television on the kitchen counter where we watch Big Bird singing about the joys of friendship. When he hangs up, he turns to Vesla at the sink. She faces him, her severe eyes pressing down on him, accusing.

Only during a seizure is the brain's activity abnormal; therefore the possibility of recording a seizure during EEG remains remote.

The next month: a new hospital, a new doctor. Mom doesn't come along to this second appointment, but when we get home she is waiting for me on my bed with a cold washcloth, a new book, and a chocolate bar. On this night, I don't need to crawl into their bed, because she lies down on my single bed with me, holding my body close.

At school I tell the other children that I am a robot and need to get recharged or else my battery will die. I make up fantastic stories about my wired insides, the maps of my computer brain, and the electrical currents that pass through my body. I explain to them that my father is the only one who understands the delicate workings of my machinery. I even begin to believe my stories a little bit. But what I don't tell the others is that I think I might be dying. It would explain why everyone in my family, except for Holly, who is too little to understand death, is being extra nice to me. I don't tell anyone that I am not afraid to die, that there is never anything on those tests.

And I hate my mother more than anything the day she stands between me and Thomas, with a hand on his chest before the third appointment, saying, "You're not taking her. It's enough, Thomas, it's over." So I call my mother a word I've never used before and she slaps me but I don't care because it figures that she'd go and keep me and Dad apart, just when I started really praying to God, asking him for the appointments to never, ever end.

Studies have revealed that gene mutations, passed on through generations, primarily through males, lead to seizure development and abnormal brain formation.

And so, with a monkey skull, hooker's swaddling on my arm, and root beer on my breath, I leap up the creaking fire escape.

—I was clean. There was nothing on the EEG, was there? A second opinion, a third . . .

We're listening for ghosts at last, my double and I, with our airtight case against love, we ascend the night alley, we go up, up!

—Still, you couldn't let it go, you couldn't be sure that I—
In search of stars, a place to rest.
—That I did belong to you, all along.

# chapter 35

We get home and Mom's in a panic: she's just phoned all the hospitals and is about to call the police.

"You think maybe she'll just come home?" she asks me.

"Sure, she'll come home, she just needs to get away from the hospital for a while, I think." She follows me around the kitchen as Sol walks into the house and arches his brows at Mom. He crushes his face into what I think is supposed to be a smile.

"Morning," Sol says, though it's almost dark. Sol dipped into more of his emergency mickey of whisky while driving home, to "cope with the current situation."

The nurse, though she looked for Giselle in laundry piles and closets, was not so helpful. Giselle's doctor called the police. I wanted to talk to them some more, but Sol, who was pacing around the halls, looked like he was really going to freak out so we left.

"Ma, Sol's got his cell, we'll call you every five minutes if you want. I think I know where she is," I lie.

"I'll go with you, I can't stand to be here, waiting."

"You have to be here in case she comes home, in case she calls, right?"

She nods slowly, absently tracing her fingers along the phone. Before she gets a chance to say anything, or stop us, I grab Sol by the arm and pull him out of the house and tell him to drive to the nearest café, slowly: I need him to sober up a bit.

Inside, I order him a double espresso while he parks the car. After I get his coffee, I stand by the doorway watching folks stroll by. There are shoppers with newly creased bags, children holding their mothers' hands. There are girls, my age, arms linked, looking in store windows, flicking down their sunglasses, licking ice cream cones and pulling their mouths into smiles. *That should be us.* Watching them, I almost believe the world is a safe and ordered place, with God still running things. I say a tiny prayer:

*Dear God, my sister needs protecting today, something from you.*

I stare down at my running shoes and then look across the street just as Sol steps in front of a car and nearly gets hit, breaking up my illusions of security. I finger the hole in Giselle's university sweatshirt; it still smells like her mango perfume. Sol's shirt is buttoned wrong, I notice. He looks at the shop, not seeing me behind the glass in the doorway. He takes big steps, the newspaper in his hand flapping in the breeze.

I step onto the street just as he is about to enter the café. And for a split second, his face lights up:

*It could be like this always, angelgirl.*

He thinks I'm her, waiting for him, ready to elope.

. . .

A crack of thunder rolls through the sky and rain starts to hit the car in hard bullets. We roll up the windows and, as if liberated by the break in heat, the electricity floats freely now, the crackling behind my ears dissolving.

I say nothing, staring out the window at an old man shuffling by in slippers with stains on his bright green shirt. He's trying to get under the canopy of a store. Sol speeds through a red light, squeaking the tires, and nearly misses a car coming from his side.

Sol's phone rings: he throws it at me, but when I pick up, the sound is chaffing, scrambled, then a click. I recognize the number.

"East end, Sol," I say quietly, trying to redial but only getting a continuous ring. I tug on Sol's jacket and he pulls away from me, and points his nose over the steering wheel like an old lady with bad eyesight.

"I heard you. How do you know where she is?"

I'm afraid to tell him that I have no idea, that it's just a hunch that Giselle is at one of our summer hangouts. She always called me from the same pay phone by the mental hospital after work, or between shifts. We'd meet on the corner next to the pay phone, where all the hookers hung out. Giselle would be waiting for me clutching a greasy bag of fries and two medium root beers. I'd have to help her up the fire escape because she was too scared to climb up by herself. She'd let me eat all her fries and then she'd smoke two cigarettes while I did cartwheels for her on the roof.

Sol hunches over the wheel and looks straight ahead. "I have a vision I can't get out of my eyes. It's been there for days now. I try to drink it away but it won't fade."

"What?"

"It's her, blue. She's lying on a sidewalk, totally, like, broken. Spaced. Gone."

"Let's check this old warehouse. We used to hang out there . . .

maybe she went up there to get some private time, away from the hospital." Sol peers at me with his bloodshot eyes, streaming now, as if the rain from outside has leaked onto his face.

The window gets fogged; he checks his shoulder to make a left turn onto the highway, then squints at the road as he accelerates.

"Who showed her how to get to the top of that place?"

Rain whips off the wipers at a steady pace; some of the cool water flies into the car, hitting him on the side of the head, cooling off the pain that burns through his skull.

"Me."

And the clouds over us turn from grey to black.

# chapter 36

A good surgeon does not submit patients to tests or rigours outside the perimeters of treatment.

It's dark from the late-afternoon rain and only a trail of yellow rimming the edge of the city indicates the sunset. Heavy in the limbs, I lie on the rooftop, trying to remember what warm feels like.

Then I close my eyes and fall under again.

Post-op reactions include: Euphoria, dysphasia, weakness, agitation, tremor, severe convulsions, uncoordinated muscle movements, transient hallucinations, disorientation, and visual disturbances.

It's almost dark now, the yellow and pink ring almost completely swallowed by grey rain clouds and night. Everything's wet, including the little pieces of gravel stuck to my arm.

—*Go on now, we're almost there.*

I inch towards the door, trying to block out her demands, trying to stay away from the edge of the roof. Finally, I reach the door, I put my hands on its smooth texture and pull myself up. There's a flash of pain as my neck reels into my spine and the cavern that once was my stomach folds over and my whole torso crushes together, like an accordion.

All sensation disappears as I extend my body up. I stretch my fingers to reach the crack between the brick and the metal door frame and I stuff my knuckles in, scraping the skin off them. Then I notice the clouds are clearing away, and see the first night's star peeking out. You would miss it if you weren't looking.

—*Where are your saviours?*

—What are you talking about?

—*Your sister, your mother, Sol?*

—They'll be here, shhhhh. Look, look at that star. Focus now.

Between the songs and shouts in my head I hear honking, music filtering in from apartments and cars. I hear girls on the phone making plans, water running in shower stalls. The sounds of night mesh together. Ice is thrown into empty glasses, promising the first of many hard-earned-end-of-day drinks.

And in night there's no longer cold, only a massive heat source lifting itself, coming up off the asphalt like some not-yet-extinct dinosaur, reclaiming its rule. My head falls back onto the top knob of my spine and I aim my eyes, again, at that one single star shining down on me as I hang on. Trying not to drop off the edge of this spinning earth, I let myself down gently and make my way to the outer lip of the roof.

—No.

As I crawl along the edge of the roof, little wet rocks adhere to my hands and face, and moist tar sticks to my palms like gum. Wet, must be soaked. The ledge cuts into my hipbone like a knife slicing into cooked steak. The vague sensation of pain helps my legs push me along the floor, over cigarette butts, glass, and pop cans. I stop to pull on my little tufts of hair, to get some feeling other than numbness inside my head. I grab on to concrete, crush rocks between my teeth, then push off with my feet and let the whole messy business of body deal with the in-between.

—*What's the name of in-between, come on now! Come on, Doctor— clavicle, cracked sarcosis, punctured lung.*

—One day they will make humans out of steel, but until then I may have to break these bones.

Then, her voice, gentle:

—*Close your eyes.*

I vomit off the roof, hear the splatter echoing on the sidewalk below. I shove my hand in my mouth to pull out the toxic flavour of greasy food and bile.

—*Thought we were on the same team, thought we . . .*

—Isn't this what you wanted? To kill me?

I punch myself in the chest to pump some air into myself. Then I haul my sorry rag of a body up onto all fours. Everywhere is wet with old rain, with mucus, and blood, and bile. Oh Papa, I'm a mess today, don't see me here. I lean over the edge, my elbows trembling, the backs of my knees covered in sweat. There's a flash and the world lights up in bone-white light, and, for an instant, I can see everything: laundry hanging in the sky, fire-escape lovers leaning on black railings, wet cats shivering in the summer rain. I see her, up above, in the middle of the sky, looking down at me.

—*Everything in this world sucks. Nothing is fun anymore.*

And just as she says this I feel the city lurch, feel it rise out of my fingertips, feel a part of it. I look down, the earth lights up again, see myself splayed below, feel my head falling forward, then I see myself seeing myself—bones scattered on this single stretch of pavement in the old city.

My head drops, heavily. I'm stuck, somehow, to the edge of the roof, sealed there with rain and sweat, my eyes roll back but I can still see things, I am almost there, on the ground below, part of the city's back. Then, from behind, I feel a blast of heat, a hand on my mouth trying to separate my clenched jaw.

—*Fuck that Solomon! He's always ruining everything.*

I am lifted up, up, up, like an already dead-thing, head knocking gently, folding into warm flesh. *I am ready,* I want to say, wrapping my arms around his solid body.

Then the cold is gone, bright light zaps against my eyelids, electric-shock synapses fizzling out like an old TV screen.

His hand grabs a handful of my hair that falls away like a cat's shedding fur into an ozone breeze. *See! I am still flesh,* I want to say, talking with my sharp teeth so that I can stay in these hard arms till morning because, for once, I don't want to die.

—*You go when I go, remember.*

—Not now, not yet.

Today I am not yet part of the earth, I'm still a little bit human. I'm not sugar and spice, not barking bones, not cracked on that sidewalk, blue, arms twisted out, bones pounded into dust, part of the city's dead, not now, not yet. I roll my eyes up, away from ground zero, see the nuclear glow of a sky rimmed with black. It's completely cloudless, and my star is not so lonely anymore.

See, it has two friends now, speckled above it, like track marks.

# chapter 37

Sol takes the last flight to the roof two steps at a time and the door bangs open from the wind before he reaches it. I jump after him, and at first we don't see anything except the yellow streaks of light in the sky and the weaving cars below us.

And then, there she is, moving like a giant worm in a wet blanket on the edge of the roof. Sol approaches her slowly.

She points to her chest and then opens her mouth but no sound comes out.

Sol picks Giselle up in the soaking blanket. She hugs his shoulders, looking at his face but not really seeing him.

"It's over, babe," he says quietly, tracing his fingers over her eyebrows.

She curls her legs over his arms, ready to be carried, while a soft rain falls on us.

. . .

At first they hooked her up to an IV, then attended to the external wounds—the scratches, the bruises, and the lung infection from exposure—and then they got down to the rest of her. Giselle has pneumonia, and it doesn't look good.

Sol drives me home in the early morning and we sit in his hot car, parked in the driveway. He lights a cigarette, then plays with the new pineapple air freshener he bought in the hospital gift shop.

When his cell rings he looks at the number and then puts his elbow on his half-open window. He clears his throat, as if he is going to say something, but he doesn't. Having him next to me makes me feel sort of normal, sort of. And I feel that what was between us before, a wire pulled taut almost breaking, is gone now, forever, at last.

Sol draws his fingers over his lips. Looking straight ahead, at our green garage, he says in a whisper, "How the hell did she do that?"

"What?"

"How did she manage to cruise around downtown, get herself halfway across the city, and onto a roof, in a goddamn thunderstorm?" He pauses to pitch his smoke out the window and turns to me. I think about how Giselle could waste a beautiful day inside, studying, how she always liked eating the heel of the bread, how I could make her laugh all day if she was hungover, and how she always did everything the hard way, never took shortcuts. Then I remember something Mom said to me once.

"People can do anything when they really want to die, Sol."

# chapter 38

Organisms that cause pneumonia are often present in the normal respiratory tract, but decreased resistance can allow these bacteria to grow unchecked, especially if immunocompromised patients are exposed to colds, flu, and emphysema.

—*You gettin' all that good juice you need?*

She comes into my room at night, tapping at the intravenous, only now she's cowed and worn, without guile, without a plan.

I nod as she crawls in bed with me.

—*Don't be afraid.*

I recoil from the cold air she lets in.

—*I'm not going to hurt you, I just wanted to say goodbye. To explain.*

I try a smile, pushing my lips together till the sores in my mouth start bleeding again.

*—Good. Because I'm not even the bad guy. G., they're trying to make me the bad guy out there.*

It is the first time she has said my name, trying to win me over now, to her side. She hitches her thumbs back over her shoulders, she pokes at the world, now it's full of recriminations, bloodlust, and injustice. The big *out-there*-world. The one I am hungry for today, at last.

—I know you're not bad, I never said you were.

I clear my throat, which feels like a blade ripping up through my lungs and into my neck.

She tries to smile against the swelling of her purple face but winces.

*—I thought you wanted out.*

—I did.

I rear up on one arm to get some air, thinking we may have run out of it there on the bed. Suddenly it all dissipates in the worst head rush I've ever had—all the cells fall away like small pieces of shattered bone. I see punctured arteries with splats of blood washing out; the cicatrice torn and spinning.

I see my two stars erupt like satellites and begin to fall. Slowly, they descend, sinking into the earth's burnt core. The nightmare of the inside turned out, the unravelling: exploding limbs, mangled flesh, cracked by the impact of bone on bone. When I look up, the sky is filled with bright blue heartsacs impaled by fire. When I look down, I see my organs torn from their holes.

*—This is what it's like . . .*

A lion-heart bursting. Entropy in reverse. It all gets messed up, the senses criss-crossed, a borderless synesthesia. A minimum of images: I see her voice, a light on the wall, then shouts churn up into one colossal, unified skipping heartbeat, tiny explosions heard from outer space.

—To die.

I finish her sentence, know that I will never be rid of her now, that I will eternally finish her thoughts.

*And I don't know anything except that—*

I am not in love with anyone anymore.

# chapter 39

Sol, Mom, Clive, and Agnes, who is chain-smoking, are all there. And Mr. Saleri is there. When I look up, I see Dad in Sol's place, standing next to Mom. She's leaning against him slightly, and he's holding her arm, shivering in his thin flannel pyjamas, bowing his head towards hers.

And Giselle is there, too, wearing a big black hat to protect her from the sun and a pink polka-dot dress I have never seen before.

I look at her, all the way in the back. She winks, gives me a thumbs-up in her black-lace gloves, and when I look at the child-size coffin in the ground and back at her, she's gone.

Then I walk away from them all.

I wobble on my black pumps on the wet ground and then kick them off and pitch them into some bushes. I start to run, the slit ripping higher and higher on Giselle's luscious black dress until my legs are free, and brown earth and grass cover my toes.

I run over graves and thorns, flowers and ashes, *Beloved Son of . . . 1968–1981 youbelovedsonofabitch,* till there's blood and muck all over my feet. I push harder then, harder, aim for the impossible spaces between bushes. I throw myself at trees, at headstones, like a human pinball in a graveyard machine. I bounce off death, off rock, off wood, the sun in my mouth, a pain scorching my breath, laughing, my thighs huge and burning. I careen back onto pavement, onto the orderly path of the living.

I fall then and roll down a hill lined with grey angels. I can hear the thud of footfalls behind me this time, boots striving to catch up with me. I hear them but they can't catch me because I'm tearing, flying, leaping over crosses like high-jump markers, landing in freshly dug graves, catching my dress and ripping it on branches.

I guess I'm screaming, too, although my voice is like the wind, too fast for sound. Still, there are those footsteps behind me but I deke them out. I fool them, hundreds of them, falling behind the sound of rolling thunder. And if I can keep this up, they won't ever catch me.

I'm too fast, too bloody. I'm on my second wind now.

# acknowledgements

In writing this book, I have consulted several sources in order to ensure the accuracy of medical terminology, surgical procedures, and certain aspects of medical training. Some passages in *Skinny* are based on material from these sources, including: *Medical School: Getting in, Staying in, Staying Human* by Keith R. Ablow (Baltimore: Williams and Watkins, 1997) and *Principles and Practice of Surgery*, 2nd ed. by C.D. Carter, A.P. Forrest, and I.B. Macleod (Edinburgh: Churchill Livingstone, 1991). For material on epilepsy, its diagnosis and treatment, I have consulted The Epilepsy Project's *www.epilepsy.com*. For statistics and procedures regarding endometriosis, I have consulted Endometriosis.org, *www.endometriosis.org*, and the MedlinePlus Medical Encyclopedia, *www.nlm.nim.gov*.

Many thanks to my editors, Iris Tupholme and Siobhan Blessing, and my agent, Don Sedgwick, for their guidance, patience, and outstanding editorship.

I would also like to acknowledge the enduring support of my family, friends, and community, whose love and faith enabled me to write this book. In particular, I would like to thank Shaughnessy Bishop-Stall, Amy Millan, Evan Cranley, Stars, Metric, the Broken, and finally, my parents, Peter and Ibolya Kaslik, for their inspiration and heart.